GUNS OF PONDEROSA

When Nate Cahill and his gang take over the town of Ponderosa, sawmill magnate Fletcher Comstock sends for his friend Matt Stryker. However, Cahill is waiting for him. He gelds Stryker's fine Arabian stallion and beats him terribly. But Stryker will not give up. He pins on the marshal's badge, tames a rowdy town and gets rid of the ruthless Cahill gang. Now the guns of Ponderosa blaze and blood runs red in the Arizona high country.

Books by Chuck Tyrell
in the Linford Western Library:

VULTURE GOLD

Please return on or before the latest date above.
You can renew online at *www.kent.gov.uk/libs*
or by telephone 08458 247 200

CHUCK TYRELL

GUNS OF PONDEROSA

Complete and Unabridged

LINFORD
Leicester

First published in Great Britain in 2010 by
Robert Hale Limited
London

First Linford Edition
published 2011
by arrangement with
Robert Hale Limited
London

British Library CIP Data

Tyrell, Chuck.
  Guns of Ponderosa. - -
  (Linford western library)
  1. Western stories.
  2. Large type books.
  I. Title II. Series
  823.9'2–dc22

  ISBN 978–1–44480–629–8

Published by
F. A. Thorpe (Publishing)
Anstey, Leicestershire

Set by Words & Graphics Ltd.
Anstey, Leicestershire
Printed and bound in Great Britain by
T. J. International Ltd., Padstow, Cornwall

This book is printed on acid-free paper

1

The Cahill gang rode into Ponderosa through the mist. Nate Cahill held the reins of his prancing blood bay in his left hand. His right rested on his thigh, inches from the butt of his single-action Colt Army .45, though his oilskin slicker was between his hand and the gun.

The five hard men angled onto Main Street. Across the way, the Comstock sawmill blew its noon whistle. The steam-driven saws screeched to a halt and the mill workers started their 30-minute noontime rest.

Main Street bustled. Two wagons stood tailgate to tailgate in front of the general store. A burly man in a canvas apron shouldered gunnysacks of grain into one. A rancher in a four-by-four hat loaded supplies into the other. Both men stopped long enough to give the five horsemen a quick glance. Nate Cahill ignored them.

The men had ridden from the Indian Nations. Cahill figured no one in Ponderosa would recognize the gang. He'd bought everyone new duds before they rode out; it wouldn't do to look like trash.

The mist dripped off Cahill's slicker and from the brim of his black Stetson. His sharp gaze picked up a comely woman in blue calico coming from a small building with *Examiner* painted on its window. Maybe she'd still be around when he owned the town. He'd see how she tasted then. Their eyes met — his cold and calculating, hers bold and forthright. Cahill raised a finger to his hat brim in salute. She looked away. He grinned.

Main Street in Ponderosa ran along the bluff overlooking the Comstock log pond, which occupied what had been a small swale in Bog Creek before Comstock Log and Lumber built a dam at the west end. Now the 300-acre

2

pond held the carcasses of ponderosa pine and Douglas fir.

At the railroad yard, Cahill took the road to Bogtown. His conquest of Ponderosa would start there.

Bogtown occupied the high land on the south side of Bog Creek, now a trickle that ran from the rock-lined spillway of Comstock Dam. Three saloons and Miss Murdock's Institute for the Redemption of Wayward Young Ladies fronted the road, which, if followed to its winding conclusion, led to the military Camp Kinishba, a dozen miles away. Cahill reined his bay up before the plank-and-batten two-storied building that housed the saloon called Old Glory.

'Reckon we'll homestead right here,' he said. The mist turned into a drizzle.

Cahill dismounted and unbuttoned his slicker, just in case. His four riders followed his example. 'You know what to do,' he said, and pushed his way into the gloomy saloon.

Wynn Cahill and the other riders

3

were only a step behind their leader as he entered. Cahill sauntered the length of the saloon and took a chair, back to the wall. Wynn sat to Cahill's left where he could watch the bar. Morales bellied up to the far end of the bar itself, and Tag and Breed stood on each side of the door to provide cover if Cahill had to leave in a hurry.

'What'll it be, gents?' the rotund barkeeper called from behind the plank bar.

'Bring your best whiskey, Holladay,' Cahill said. 'And get Bart Sims out here.'

'Do I know you boys?' The barkeep's face wore a puzzled frown.

'Just bring the damned whiskey.'

Jake Holladay pulled a bottle of Turley's Mill from the hutch and took it to Cahill's table with two cloudy glasses. 'Here ya go,' he said, his voice oozing bonhomie.

'Get Sims.'

'Yes, sir. Who should I say's asking for him?'

'The new owner of Old Glory,' Cahill said.

Holladay stared at Cahill.

'Move!' Cahill roared.

The barkeep scrambled through the back door and his footsteps pounded up a flight of stairs.

Cahill filled a shot glass with Turley's Mill. 'You boys can have a drink as soon as this business with Sims is over,' he said. He tossed the amber whiskey back and shuddered. The 90-proof liquor burned its pleasurable way down his throat and into his guts. Fumes from the potent whiskey filled his nose and made his eyes water. 'Damn good whiskey, this Turley's Mill. Be worth the wait,' Cahill said. He swallowed the saliva that flooded his mouth. It was almost like taking another shot.

An angry voice came through the thin walls. 'He's what? You're jerking my leg. I'm the goddam owner of this goddam saloon.' Angry stomps marked Sims's progress down the stairs. He burst into the room, a big man in

5

gartered sleeves and suspenders. His belly hung over his waistband and jowls flapped at his neck. He held a Smith & Wesson in his right hand.

'Who the hell are you?' he shouted. The revolver pointed more or less at Cahill.

'I'm Nate Cahill, and this here's my brother Wynn. Now before you get sudden, let me tell you about Wynn. He's not like other people. You see, Wynn likes to hurt things. Cats, Dogs. Women. Men. Don't matter much to him, long as they yowl.'

'So what? I'm the one holding this here S 'n' W. Don't even have to cock the damn thing either, just pull the gawdawful trigger. Shit. Likes to hurt things.'

Wynn showed a feral grin that bared teeth as sharp and pointed as fangs. His breath hissed out from between lips as thin and colorless as a sidewinder's.

Involuntarily, Sims took a step back. His arm began to swing up as if of its own accord, bringing the double-action revolver into line. Wynn shot him just above the knee from beneath the table.

The big lead bullet smashed into Sims's thigh bone and drove him backwards. The Smith & Wesson flew from his hand as his arms windmilled and he crashed into the bar. He came to rest with his back against the bar's frontpiece and his legs spraddled. Blood ran in rivulets from beneath the ruined left leg.

'Jesus. Jesus. Mary, Mother of God. Holy Father.' Sims clutched his leg above the wound, but the blood still ran. 'Help. Please. God.' He pleaded.

Wynn scraped his chair back from the table and holstered his Colt. He casually walked around the table and dug a boot toe into Sims's leg wound.

Sims screamed.

'Oh, sorry. Did I hurt you?' Wynn's toe probed the wound again.

'Aaargh. Doctor. God. Help.' Tears streamed down Sims's face. 'Oh, please. I'm bleeding. My leg's broke. Get Doc Huntly. Oh G-g-g-god.'

'Get him to sign the quit claim,' Cahill said. He pushed a folded sheet of paper across the table to Wynn.

'*Señor*. Don't try. *Por favor*. Place your hands on the bar where I can see them,' Morales said to the barkeep, who may have been contemplating a dive for his shotgun.

Wynn unfolded the paper and held out his hand. Cahill pulled a turkey quill from his hat and trimmed it to a point with his clasp knife. He handed the improvised pen to Wynn.

'What do I use for ink?'

'He's bleeding pretty good,' Cahill said. 'Use that.'

Wynn nudged Sims's shattered leg again. Sims screamed. Wynn leaned over and waved the paper in front of Sims's face. 'Hey, Mister Sims,' he said. 'Can you see this? It says you gave Old Glory to my brother Nate for . . . value rendered. You sign and we'll send for the doc.'

Sims moaned.

Wynn dragged a chair over and

spread the quit claim out on its seat. He dipped the quill in the blood welling from Sims's leg. He slapped Sims's face. The owner's eyes sprang open. 'Sign,' Wynn said. 'Live.'

Sims was hardly able to take the quill. He squinted at the paper, held it down with his left hand, and scrawled his signature across the bottom in blood.

'That's right,' Wynn said. He passed the quit claim back to Nate.

'Doctor,' Sims croaked. 'D-d-d-doctor.' He tried feebly to stop the flow of blood with his gore-covered hands.

'Let me get Mister Sims some help,' Holladay said. 'Please.'

Wynn Cahill turned his serpent's stare on Holladay, showed his feral smile, and shot the bartender through the left eye. The bullet tore a chunk of bone from the back of Holladay's head and plowed into the plank wall not two inches from the plate glass mirror behind the bar.

The bartender smashed against the

wall and crumpled into a lifeless heap.

Wynn nudged Sims's wounded leg with a boot toe. Almost no response. 'Leave him like that,' Cahill said. 'He's about bled out. We got what we came for.' His conquest of Ponderosa had gotten off to an excellent start.

★ ★ ★

Two days later, Bogtown knew the Cahills had taken over Old Glory. A week later, the saloon sported a new paint job, a roulette wheel, a tall skinny barkeep with a tick in one cheek, and a card shark who divided his winnings with the house. Nate Cahill informed Bucktooth Alice Murdock that Tag Riddle would 'protect' her customers for a dollar a head, and Tag moved into a chair in Alice's parlor, where he sat with a long-barreled 10-gauge across his knees. At closing time, Tag collected the protection money and delivered it to Nate Cahill.

With soldiers in town and sawyers off

work, Old Glory rattled on its foundations.

The roulette wheel clicked to a stop. 'Red seven,' the operator intoned.

'Yee-Haw! I'm king of the mountain and I ain't begun to roll.' A young cowboy raked a pile of chips over. 'Holy roller,' he said, hands steepled before his face. 'One more time.' He divided his chips. Then, 'Aw, hell with it. Put it all on red again.'

Word traveled around the room like a prairie fire before the wind. 'Richie Brown's riding on red — ' Bluecoats and sawyers gathered round.

'Any more bets, gentlemen?' The operator nodded and set the wheel in motion. He took one more look at the players and then flicked the white ball onto the spinning wheel. The saloon went quiet as the ball clicked its way around. It came to rest on red 27 and the room erupted.

Nate Cahill fired a round into the ceiling and the bedlam dropped to a murmur. The operator handed him a piece of paper. Cahill held it up. 'Gentlemen,' he shouted. 'Old Glory's right proud to announce the biggest winner she's ever had.' He gestured toward the cowboy. 'Mister Richie Brown of the Bar B Bar. He put the whole wad on red and damn near broke the house. Now I owe him five thousand five hundred and fifty-five dollars — exactly.' Cahill turned to the winner. 'Mr Brown. Let me buy you a drink.'

'You're a big man, Mr Cahill,' the cowboy said. 'I'll take that drink, and I'll buy one for you and everyone else in the place!'

Suddenly men stood four and five deep at the bar, hands outstretched for free drinks. Cahill steered Brown to his table in the back. 'Looks like everybody's happy about your generosity, son. We'll charge you by the bottle — cheaper that way. Have a seat.' Cahill crooked a finger at Breed, who stood guard at the rear door, shotgun in hand.

'Jigger can't hear in this noise, Breed.

Could you get the special bottle from his stock for Mr Brown?'

Breed nodded and shouldered his way behind the bar. He returned with a bottle full of pale liquor.

'Don't look like prime whiskey to me,' Brown said.

'You're absolutely right, Mr Brown. It ain't whiskey, it's rum and it's goldam over 100 proof and it'll knock your socks right off your feet if you can't hold your liquor. Want to try it?'

'More'n a hunnert proof, eh?'

'A lot more.'

'Ye-e-e-e-e ha-a-a-aw! Pour that sumbitch. Let's get to drinking.'

Cahill filled Brown's glass with rum, 140 proof. He held up his own, full of whiskey.

'Ain't you having none of this rum?'

'Can't handle it, to tell the truth. Getting too old, I reckon,' Cahill said.

Brown grinned. 'Well, OK. Down the hatch she goes.' He tossed a double shot of the potent rum.

'Whoooo-ee. That's some firewater,'

the cowboy said.

Cahill refilled Brown's glass, and kept refilling it. When Old Glory closed, Richie Brown still sat at the rear table, glassy-eyed and unable to move.

★ ★ ★

Marshal Braxton Webber pushed through Old Glory's batwing doors, a stocky man with graying hair and middle-age spread. He wore a Colt Peacemaker on his right hip, covered by his black frock coat. A sawed-off shotgun hung from the crook of his arm.

The skinny barkeep stood behind the bar and Wynn Cahill sat at the Cahill table in the back of the long room.

Webber stopped just inside the door to let his eyes adjust to the dim interior. The sober look on his face said he wasn't just calling to see neighbors. The wrinkles in his nose indicated he might not like the odors of old sweat, sour beer, puke, and fresh sawdust that formed the ambience of Old Glory. He brushed the tail of his frock coat back behind the Peacemaker.

Wynn slipped the thong from the hammer of his own Peacemaker. No telling when a lawman would pick a fight.

Webber looked at Jigger the barkeep. 'Get Nate Cahill in here,' he said.

Jigger glanced at Wynn for instructions.

'Now what would the law want with my law-abiding brother?' Wynn asked.

'Stick around, you'll find out.' Webber turned to look at the barman once more. 'Get him. Tell him Brax Webber's come calling.'

Wynn jerked his head toward the back door.

'Yes, sir, Marshal. I'll get him.' Jigger fled through the door to find Cahill.

In the silence, the whine of the big steam saws at Comstock seemed to draw closer. Webber stood stock still, feet apart, as if primed for a shootout on some dusty street. Wynn Cahill licked his lips. It'd been too long since

15

he'd got to kill Sims. He was starting to get thirsty for blood again. He stared at the marshal and wondered how he'd stand up to a little pain.

Jigger trotted back in and took a position behind the bar. 'Mister Cahill will be here directly,' he said. 'Would you like something to drink?'

One corner of Webber's mouth twitched in a sardonic grin. 'Sure,' he said. 'Gimme a sarsaparilla.'

'Ain't got none.'

Webber nodded. 'Thought not. Whiskey rots the mind, you know. Be careful how you drink.'

Silence. The three men waited for Cahill to appear. Jigger fidgeted, then wiped the bar with a damp rag. Wynn was motionless. So was Webber.

The upstairs door slammed and boots clomped down the stairs. Nate Cahill entered in a white planter's hat, gray frock coat, white shirt, maroon silk cravat, pearl-gray trousers, and leather boots. His hair curled about his collar, glistening with pomade. He was the picture of prosperity. Cahill glanced at his men — Wynn at the table, Jigger at the bar, Morales against the far wall, Breed slouched on a bar stool — all set. Cahill stopped, spraddle-legged, just at the foot of the stairs. To look at him, a man would think Cahill was unarmed. He wore a smile on his face as he spoke. 'You want me for something, Webber?'

'Depends.'

'On what?'

'When you last saw Richie Brown.'

Cahill frowned. 'Richie Brown? He damned near broke me last night. Thank God he bought a round or two for the boys. We got to make a little back. He was here till closing. Don't know what happened after that. He was fairly well drunk when he left here, though.' Cahill shrugged. 'That's about all I can say, Webber.'

Webber heaved the shotgun into his hand. It pointed at the space between Cahill and Wynn. 'Seems funny to me,' he said, 'that Richie would end up floating face down in the Comstock log pond this morning, don't you?'

Cahill's eyebrows shot up. 'The log pond, you say. That'd make for soggy greenbacks, I'd say.'

'No greenbacks on him.'

'Robbery?'

'All I'm saying is, Richie's dead.'

Cahill shrugged again. 'Well, that's sad, Webber, but I don't see how that has anything to do with me or Old Glory.'

'Cahill. The fact that Richie won big here last night and turned up dead in the log pond this morning seems almighty coincidental to me,' Webber said.

Cahill laughed. 'Webber, half the people in Bogtown would cut their own grandmother's throat for a double eagle. Gambling's part of my business. We win some; we lose some. It all comes out in the end.'

'You're almighty jolly for a man who had to shell out a cartload of cash last night.' The shotgun still aimed at a spot between Wynn and Nate Cahill.

Wynn sneered. 'You waving that scattergun around just to scare us Cahills?'

'Just playing things safe,' Webber said. 'Cahill, you mind my taking a look in that safe you got on the second floor?'

'Can't do that, Webber. You got no right.'

Webber took a deep breath. 'I'm the one with the badge, Cahill. This may be Bogtown, but it's still part of Ponderosa, and I'm the law.'

Cahill smirked. 'That so? You figure there's some way to make me open that safe for you?'

'There is.' Webber eared back the hammers of the sawed-off shotgun, but the moment the marshal's hand moved to the hammers, Wynn Cahill palmed his Colt and shot Webber just below the breastbone. Webber stumbled backwards. His dying fingers triggered the shotgun into the ceiling. He fell on his back, his head crashing on the hardwood floor.

The Cahills watched as the marshal tried to suck air into his punctured lungs while his dying heart pumped blood out his ruptured pulmonary artery into his chest cavity. His heels beat a weak tattoo on the floor; then he went limp.

'Damn,' Wynn said. 'Why'd he have to die so quick?'

2

Matt Stryker reined his Arabian stallion to a stop in front of the county courthouse in Yuma. He sat in the saddle a moment and scrutinized the adobe building. Sheriff Andy Tyner had an office in there and Stryker was bound to deliver to Tyner the body of Crazy Bill Dent, shrouded in a ground cloth and draped over the saddle of a shaggy brown horse. Cold and stiff as it was, the corpse was still worth a thousand dollars. Stryker wanted nothing more than to be rid of the gruesome load so he could get a shave and a bath and a new suit of clothes.

'Boy,' he called to a youngster rolling a hoop down the street.

The boy caught the hoop with his stick. 'Whatcha got on that other horse?' he asked.

'Dead man,' Stryker said.

'No guff?'

'Deader than an ear-shot hog.'

The boy took a step back and watched the corpse from the corner of his eye.

'Do you want to earn a dime?'

'A whole dime? What do I gotta do?'

'Run into the sheriff's office and tell him Matt Stryker's here with Crazy Bill, OK?'

The boy dashed into the building before Stryker could change his mind. Stryker fished a bag of Bull Durham from his shirt pocket, found a paper, and rolled a smoke. He lit it with a lucifer and looked up in time to see the sheriff come out the courthouse door, squinting against the brilliant Arizona sunlight. The boy tagged in Tyner's footsteps. Stryker dragged on the cigarette and savored the biting, acrid smoke.

Tyner lifted the canvas that covered Crazy Bill's face. 'That's him, all right.'

'Can you take the corpse off my hands, Sheriff? I'm tired of hauling it around.' Stryker held out the reins of the dead man's horse.

'Just take Crazy over to Jim Beckworth's, would you? I'll have your voucher ready when you get back.' Without waiting for Stryker's answer, the sheriff turned on his heel and left him with an odoriferous dead body to deliver to the undertaker. The boy stood still, his eyes on Stryker's face. Stryker fingered a coin from his vest pocket. 'Much obliged, kid,' he said, and flipped the dime to the boy.

'Thanks, mister,' the boy shouted at Stryker's receding back, but the man in black didn't answer.

★ ★ ★

'Man! I get two hundred for going all the way to Tucson to pick up a jailbreaker and you clear a thousand. Somehow it don't seem fair.' Andy Tyner handed the bank draft to Stryker with a big smile on his face.

Stryker folded the draft and put it

23

away. 'Thanks, Sheriff. If Crazy Bill hadn't got on the wrong side of all those ranchers in Cheyenne, he'd not have been worth a hundred.'

Tyner mopped his perspiring face with a blue bandanna. 'Hot enough to fry horny toads,' he said.

Stryker offered a slim smile. Though he wore black over white and gray, he rarely broke a sweat. He reckoned it might have something to do with his plantation upbringing. 'Yes, quite warm,' he said. 'What lucrative dodgers might you have today, Sheriff?'

Tyner reached into a bottom drawer and brought out a double handful of Wanted sheets. 'Here. Help yourself. Only a couple new and they ain't worth much.'

The boy with the barrel hoop stuck his head in the door. He took a swallow to help him catch his breath. He looked at Stryker from the corners of his eyes as if he were afraid of the big man.

'What's up, Robby?' the sheriff said.

'Well . . . I mean . . . I was over to the

station talking to Jenks and I told him about that dead man, that Crazy Bill, and he wanted to know who cotch him and I told him it were Matt Stryker and he sat up in his chair all straight and surprised and he said, 'Why, I've been holding a telegram for Mr Stryker,' and I volunteered to deliver the telegram because I knowed Mr Stryker personal and . . . well . . . here it is.' He held out the yellow Western Union form toward Stryker.

'Who would be wiring me?' Stryker mused.

'Fletcher Comstock, Mr Stryker,' the boy said.

Stryker gave the boy a sharp look and a faint smile. 'Fletcher Comstock, eh? What would he want with me, I wonder?'

'Wants you to be marshal up to Ponderosa,' the boy said.

Stryker's brows shot up and he barked a laugh. 'Do you always read messages addressed to others?'

'Oh no, sir, well, not usually, er, um,

25

yes, sir, mostly I do.' The boy scrubbed the oiled wood floor with a bare toe.

Stryker unfolded the yellow telegram.

URGENT U CUM PNDRSA
BE MRSHL
100 A MONTH N FINES STOP
F COMSTOCK

A faraway look came to Stryker's eyes as he stared out the window across the Colorado River toward California. He owed Comstock for Virginia City. 'Reckon I'll ride for Ponderosa,' he said. 'Best turn a man down in person.'

* * *

'Stryker's coming.' Word spread through Ponderosa like lightning fire through dry jack pines.

'That's Stryker,' women whispered on the boardwalk in front of the general store as the tall man rode past. They noticed his black frock coat was hitched back to uncover the ivory stocks of an

Army Colt. They saw the straight-brimmed Stetson pulled low over slits of eyes in which cold blue ice glittered. They eyed the brocaded vest, the striped California britches, the golden-yellow cravat, and the polished riding boots mounted with spurs that had no rowels, just small golden knobs.

Matt Stryker ignored the gathering crowd. He'd come to decline Fletcher Comstock's job offer. That's all.

The stallion pranced as a wagon passed. His headstall and saddle gleamed like Stryker's boots. The horse seemed proud to bear his rider. 'Stop, Saif,' Stryker said, and the Arabian halted at a hitching rail. The sign said Comstock Hotel. It seemed a likely place to look for Fletcher Comstock. Stryker dismounted, leaving the reins looped over the small saddle horn, and climbed the steps to the hotel's front door. People parted at his approach.

'Don't you dare touch me!'

Stryker turned at the strident tone. Three men had a young woman cornered on the boardwalk.

'Boss wants to talk to you,' said one of the men.

'I have no intention of talking to Nate Cahill, and you can relay that message, Tag Riddle.'

The big man called Tag Riddle took the woman by the forearm. 'Boss says you're to come.'

'Let go of me!'

A Mexican-looking man reached for her other arm. '*Pardon*, miss. *El patron*. He insists.'

The third man stood against the wall, arms folded, stoic.

The woman screeched.

Stryker moved swiftly, drawing his Colt as he strode toward the men. Tag Riddle turned at the approach of Stryker's footsteps just in time to take the barrel of Stryker's pistol across the side of his head. He dropped in a heap. On the back swing, Stryker's gun came down on the crown of the Mexican's hat. He dropped to his haunches, holding his head in his hands.

The pound of running feet came from up the boardwalk, as a man with a star on his vest came rushing toward the group.

'Are you all right, miss?' Stryker took the woman's elbow.

She jerked away. 'Don't you touch me either, or I'll have the law on you.'

Stryker showed his half-smile. 'Heard there was no law in Ponderosa,' he said.

'He's the law,' she said, pointing at the approaching man with a star. 'That's Deputy Marshal Dan Brady.'

Brady skidded to a halt, nearly out of breath. 'What's the ruckus?'

'The young lady is all right. Does that star on your pocket mean anything?'

Hardly more than a boy, the man with the star couldn't meet Stryker's hard eyes. Blond hair leaked from under his sweat-stained hat. His blue work shirt and well-worn Levis topped a pair of mule-ear boots run over at the heels. The man gulped, but the girl spoke. 'I said he was Dan Brady, our

29

deputy marshal, mister.'

'And who might the marshal be?'

The young deputy finally recovered his power of speech. 'Brax Webber got killed in Bogtown ten days ago,' he said.

'Hmm, well, these men were trying to do this woman harm. Throw them in jail.'

Brady pulled an enormous converted Dragoon Colt. 'Yes, sir,' he said. He prodded the big man with a toe. 'Get up, Riddle. You, too, Morales.' The ruffians struggled to their feet. 'Let's go. You all got a nice comfortable cell waiting. Begging your pardon, Miss Prudence.'

Stryker still held the Colt in his right hand. He nailed the man against the wall with his cold blue stare. 'Are you with them?' Stryker nodded toward the ruffians.

'We ride together sometimes.'

'Name?'

'They call me Breed.'

'You didn't help.'

'Don't cotton much to bothering women.'

Stryker nodded. 'Go tell your boss what happened.'

'He'll already know.'

'You ride with that kind, you ride into trouble. Mind yourself, Breed.'

The dark man nodded, then stepped away.

'May I escort you somewhere, miss?' Stryker asked the woman.

'I'm perfectly able to fend for myself,' she said, tossing her head.

Stryker gave her a thin smile. 'Yes, I saw how well you did that a moment ago.'

'Matt!'

Stryker turned toward the hotel doorway. He smiled. 'I came here just to talk with you, Fletcher,' he said.

'Glad you're here, by God. We need you!' Fletcher Comstock looked like a lumberjack fresh from the woods. Stryker couldn't help wondering if there were sawdust in the lumber magnate's hair. Lumber magnate. Back in Virginia City, Stryker had been a green lawman and Comstock a lean prospector with big dreams. The two were the only ones left of a ten-man posse that chased a bunch of Piutes. But between them, they survived.

'Where should we talk?' Stryker asked.

'My office?'

'Any coffee?'

Comstock grinned. 'We'll get some,' he said. 'Come on.'

'Stay, Saif,' Stryker said to his stallion, and left the horse standing in front of the Comstock Hotel. Stryker went into Clark's Kitchen next to the hotel to wait while Comstock drummed up a pot of coffee and two earthenware mugs.

In Fletcher Comstock's office, the two men sipped Arbuckle's finest for a while without speaking.

'Got your wire in Yuma,' Stryker said at last.

Comstock searched Stryker's eyes. 'I sent telegrams all over the by-God country,' he said. 'Figured you'd run into one somewhere.'

'Can't do it, Fletcher.'

'What?'

'Marshal your town.'

'You saw what it's like around here. Dan Brady just ain't got the right stuff. What I mean is, he's all right as a deputy, but he can't make rannies into law-abiding folks all by himself.'

'I'm not your man, Fletcher. There's a bunch of lawmen who could do better. Bill Breckenridge would be good. I hear Johnny Behan's out of a job right now. Or one of the Earp brothers. Tombstone doesn't need all three of them. With your lumber and the rail spur up here like this, you got a good town going, Fletcher. Get yourself a good lawman, not a bounty hunter.'

Comstock stared at the table, took a sip of coffee, heaved a long sigh, and lifted his eyes to Stryker's. 'Matt,' he said, 'you're the hardest man I know. Honest to a fault. No give. No back down. And you've worn a star before. You're what Ponderosa needs if we're going to grow up.'

33

Stryker slowly shook his head. 'No, I'm not, Fletcher. You need a man who cares. I just don't give a damn. I do my part by tracking down those with prices on their heads and putting them out of circulation.'

'Mighty risky business.'

'Like I said. I just don't give a damn. Those carpetbaggers killed my Martha and burned me out. Nothing left for me to give a damn about. Never again. No, Fletcher. I can't accept your offer.'

'Damn. Double damn.' Comstock sighed again, then lifted the coffee pot. 'We might as well finish off the coffee before you go.'

Stryker smiled his thin smile. 'Glad you understand, Fletcher,' he said, holding out his cup. 'Excellent coffee, that.'

Comstock pleaded no more. And Stryker, stubborn in his own right, was happy the lumberman didn't keep jabbing.

'You go ahead, Matt,' Comstock said when the coffee was gone. 'I've got paperwork to do, by God. Seems I never get finished.'

Stryker stood and carefully placed his Stetson on his head. 'Thanks, Fletcher,' he said. 'I'd like to help, but I'm not the right man. I reckon you know that.'

Comstock waved his hand. 'Can't force you to do something you don't feel right about,' he said.

As Stryker left the Comstock Log and Lumber Company, he heard Saif scream in hurt and anger. Stryker broke into a run. The stallion screamed again, and the sound of breaking wood and shouting cowboys came as Stryker pounded down the gravelled street. The cowboys were waiting for Stryker. As he rounded the corner, a loop dropped over his head and pinned his arms to his sides. Saif was down and kicking, but a cowboy with a bloody knife shouted, 'Got the damned thing,' and waved a bloody testicle above his head. The cowboy with the rope jerked Stryker off his feet and loped his pony down the hillside toward Bogtown,

35

dragging Stryker behind.

The cavalcade of cowboys grouped in front of Old Glory. Stryker struggled to his feet in time for two more loops to drop over his head and pin him in a three-way bind. Nate Cahill stepped through the batwing doors of Old Glory, drawing on a pair of doeskin gloves. 'Heard you buffaloed two of my men, Stryker,' he said. 'Can't have you doing that in my town.'

Stryker stopped struggling to pin Cahill with his ice-blue stare.

Cahill grinned. 'Don't give me the evil eye, Stryker. Time I finish, you're gonna wish you never even heard of Ponderosa.' Cahill wrapped his hand around a bar of lead specially fitted to the inside of his fist. He lifted Stryker's chin with the fingers of his left hand and smashed his right into Stryker's face, crushing the cheekbone.

Stryker grunted. 'Do your damndest, Cahill. But you'd better kill me. If you don't, you won't be able to sleep nights. You'll never know when I'll be there.'

'The hell you say. You. Stay. Out. Of. My. Town.' With each word, Cahill smashed a lead-filled fist into Stryker's face, pulverizing bone and tearing flesh.

The cowboys had to hold Stryker up as Cahill beat him a final dozen blows. The bounty hunter's face was bruised, battered, and broken beyond recognition.

'Bring his horse,' Cahill rasped, his breath coming in gasps.

The cowboys towed the half-castrated Arabian at the end of half a dozen lariats. The big horse fought and screamed until a broncbuster eared him down. They tied Stryker into the saddle, facing backwards. Somehow he was able to sit up, though his eyes were swollen shut and his jaw was at an angle.

'This is my town, Stryker. You remember that, or next time the penalty will be more severe,' Cahill said. 'This is my town!'

Cahill pulled off his white planter's hat. 'Turn the horse loose.' The broncbuster let the stallion up and Cahill slapped him across the rump with the big hat. The Arabian lit out on a dead run with Matt Stryker clinging to the saddle, backwards. Cowboy laughter followed him as Saif ran down Corduroy Road toward Camp Kinishba.

3

Stryker met Tom Hall at Cory Cooley's White House. The gunman stepped lightly through the door and moved left along the wall. Stryker gave him time to let his eyes adjust to the dim interior, then waved Hall over.

'Sit and have some coffee, Tom.' Stryker's voice rasped, low and husky, almost a whisper.

'My God, what happened to your face?'

'That's part of it,' Stryker said, fingering the lumps of scar tissue on his right cheek.

'OK, what's going down?'

Stryker told him what happened in Ponderosa. 'Right now, Nate Cahill thinks he's King of the Mountain in that town. I turned Fletcher Comstock down when he asked me to tame the town, then those rowdies roped and beat me, and half-gelded Saif. The time has come to make Ponderosa a respectable place, and I need you to watch my back.'

Tom Hall leaned back in his chair. 'Pay?'

'Five hundred out front and half any fines we levy,'

Hall whistled. 'I ain't worth that kind of money.'

'Tom, Cahill's got a nasty bunch in Ponderosa. I want one man I can trust to do the right thing when the cards are all on the table. I don't spend much money drinking and such, and I've got a bit socked away. It'll be worth the money to me to have you back me up.'

'Tell you what. I'll take two hundred now and we'll see when the job's finished if you owe me anything.'

Stryker thrust out a hand and Tom Hall shook it.

★ ★ ★

Fletcher Comstock pored over ledgers in the yellow light of a coal-oil lamp.

40

Three more shipments of ponderosa pine lumber would give him the money for another steam saw and a planer mill.

The sound of boot heels in the hallway took Comstock's attention to the door. Who could it be, this time of night? Where was the night watchman? Before he could call for the night man, Nate Cahill stepped into the doorway and leaned against the frame.

'Midnight oil, eh, Comstock?'

'None of your by-God business, Cahill.'

'You're wrong, Comstock, dead wrong. Now, we've been without a marshal for nigh on to a month. Things are getting almighty lawless around. Like I said, it's time we had us a marshal.' Cahill grinned at Comstock's discomfort. He plucked the makings from a vest pocket and rolled a cigarette. He stepped across to the desk to light the smoke over the chimney of the lamp. He drew deeply, then blew the smoke in Comstock's direction. 'I'll tell you what I'll do, Comstock. You all ain't invited me to join the Ponderosa Club, but I'll still donate a good man to be marshal, and you can bet he'll have plenty of back-up.' Cahill pulled a Colt from his waistband, cocked it, and laid it on the desk, muzzle pointed at Comstock's chest. 'I don't want your sawmill, Comstock. I just want a good safe town to do my business in. Now give me that marshal's badge.'

Comstock stared at Cahill for a long moment. Then opened the middle drawer of his desk.

'When your hand comes out of there, it better not be holding a gun,' Cahill said.

Comstock said nothing, but his face showed his disgust. 'If I thought it would solve anything,' he said, 'I'd walk through your cocked Colt and strangle you with my bare hands.' His hand appeared, holding a star-in-a-circle badge with MARSHAL stamped on it. He tossed it on the desk. 'You take the badge, Cahill. But let me warn you. It's going to bring you grief like you never had in your whole life. Count on it.'

Cahill pocketed the star. 'Won't be

me wearing it,' he said.

'Be you that gets the grief, though.'

'Aw, shut up. You run your sawmill and I'll run the town. Get that?'

Comstock said nothing.

Cahill picked up the Colt and pressed its muzzle against Comstock's forehead. 'Get that?' he repeated.

Comstock stared at him without a word.

* * *

Tag Riddle wore the badge and Ponderosa turned into the rowdiest town north of Tombstone. It didn't have the gold of Vulture City or the copper of Bisbee, but the Comstock sawmill's lumberjacks and sawyers, Camp Kinishba's blue-coated soldiers, and cowboys from ranches scattered through the foothills of the White Mountains from the Mogollon Rim to the badlands in New Mexico converged on Ponderosa to gamble and carouse. Mostly the rowdies stayed across the creek in Bogtown to have their fun, but they sometimes strutted on Main Street, too.

Marshal Riddle opened one eye as Herbert Gardner charged into the marshal's office, his face livid. Flour streaked his hair and dusted his shirt and apron. 'Marshal! You've got to do something.'

'I am. Right now, I'm busy keeping the peace.'

'You are not. You're sleeping on the job.'

Riddle opened his other eye. 'Are you telling me how to do my job?' His voice carried the threat of violence.

'Er, oh, no, I wouldn't do that, Marshal. It's just that those Bar B Bar cowboys are having a flour fight in my store.'

Riddle laughed. 'Sounds like it might be amusing. Can't see where flour'd break things. You just stand back out of the way and let them have their fun. They'll go back down to Old Glory when they run out of booze.'

Gardner's shoulders sagged. 'I should have known,' he said, and dragged his feet as he went out the door.

'Why didn't we help him?' Dan Brady asked.

'Why should we?'

'We're the law. We're supposed to help the people in this town, right?'

Riddle sneered. 'Do what? Help who?'

'Well, ain't laws supposed to protect them what can't use a gun or knife to protect themselves?'

Riddle swivelled to face the deputy. 'See here, Brady. I got this badge from Nate Cahill. I do what makes him happy. Them cowboys cutting up in Gardner's store ain't no skin off the boss's nose. By 'n' by, they'll wander back to Bogtown where the boss wants them.'

Brady couldn't meet Riddle's angry eyes.

'You all just be glad you still got a job. The boss coulda fired your ass, you know.'

Brady dug a boot toe at a stain on the floor. He didn't raise his eyes; he didn't speak.

'You hearing me, kid?'

Brady nodded.

Morales stuck his head in the door. 'Boss wants you.'

'All the way to Bogtown?'

'Over to the general store.'

'Shit.' Riddle buckled on his gunbelt as he left the office. 'You stay here,' he said to Brady.

Nate Cahill stood just inside the door of the general store when Riddle and Morales rushed in.

'Boss?' Riddle said.

Cahill swept his arm at the room. 'Look at this mess, Marshal.'

The contents of at least a barrel of flour covered Gardner's goods and lay thick on the floor. A fine white dust still clung in the air. Three cowboys, liberally decorated in white, stood in a line at the counter, swaying slightly on unsteady legs.

'Just some high-spirited cowboys,

boss,' Riddle said. 'No harm done.'

Cahill shook his head. His oiled curls danced beneath his hat. 'Oh no, Marshal, this kind of thing should not be allowed to happen. Don't you agree?'

'Uh, well, of course you're right, boss, of course.'

'Mr Gardner.' Cahill beckoned the storeowner over. 'Marshal Riddle can't do much about what has already happened, and it takes men and money to lay down the law to the whole town. But I think that if you were to help foot some of the bill, say thirty dollars a month, that'd go a long way towards keeping skylarking cowboys from dusting your goods with flour like this.' Cahill waved his arm at the flour-splotched goods again. 'Wouldn't thirty a month help, Marshal?'

Riddle started. 'Oh, yeah, boss, that'd be real fine.'

Cahill showed Gardner his feral smile. 'Of course, if you can't see fit to contribute, who knows what those

fun-loving rannies will do to your
. . . establishment.'

Gardner's mouth hung open.

'Ah, you'll want to think about what
I've said. All right. The marshal will come
by in the morning for your answer. I'll
leave you to the job of cleaning up.'

Outside, Cahill said, 'He'll pay. I can
see it in his eyes. You collect tomorrow,
Riddle. And bring the money straight to
Old Glory, y'hear.'

Riddle laughed. 'Boss, you're better'n
anything I ever saw. This beats the hell
outta hitting trains.'

By the end of the week, every
business in Ponderosa paid Nate Cahill
for protection against rabble-rousers;
every business, that is, except Comstock Log and Lumber Company.

★ ★ ★

A tap came at Fletcher Comstock's bedroom window. His lapstrake whitewashed
house stood back from Ash Street in a
grove of ponderosa and spruce.

48

'No lights,' a gravelly voice said, and Comstock obeyed. He lifted the window, which he found by feel. A huge black shape loomed, and Comstock stepped back.

'It's me, Fletcher,' the voice said.

'What in hell . . . Matt?'

'Yes, Fletcher. Matt Stryker.'

'In the middle of the by-God night? Are you running from the law?'

'No, I'm not running, Fletcher. I've got debts to pay in Ponderosa.'

'You never spend money. What do you mean, debts?'

'I reckon you heard about Nate Cahill running me out of town riding my own horse backwards?'

'I heard.'

'He did that to me, Fletcher.' The rasp of Stryker's voice seemed to deepen. 'And I can't let him get away with it.'

'Are you going to kill him?'

'If I must.'

'W-what? How?'

The dark shape leaned closer. Comstock

strained to see in the black shadows, but saw only darkness.

'Is that marshal job still open?'

'Tag Riddle's wearing the badge.'

'Is the job still open?'

'Cahill runs the town.'

'Fletcher? Is that you?'

'Yeah. Why?'

'Doesn't sound like you. Sounds like a quitter.'

Comstock said nothing.

'Is that right? Are you buffaloed?'

Comstock remained silent.

'Well I'll be damned. The man who chewed cactus all the way back to Virginia City's got faint. I'd have never reckoned that.'

Comstock stirred. 'It's not that, Matt. But I've got more than twenty grand tied up in that mill. I'd just as soon not get it burned down.'

'Fletcher, I'm going to take Cahill's little castle apart, starting with the marshal's office. I'd hoped for your support, but I'll do without it if I have to.'

'You know I'll do what I can,' Comstock said, then the shadow was gone. He stood for a long moment, listening to the soughing of the pines. *What will Matt Stryker bring to Ponderosa*, he wondered. He listened hard at the open window, but heard nothing. Damn. Sure, no one wanted to be strongarmed by someone like Nate Cahill. But now that everyone paid for protection, unruly cowboys and sawyers and soldiers stayed across the creek in Bogtown for the most part. Now Stryker had to come along and threaten to turn things upside down. Comstock's operation, well, all the businesses in town for that matter, depended on the peace being kept. Cahill saw to it that rowdies didn't get out of hand. That helped business. Most made much more than the few dollars they paid for protection . . . no, paid to help the law keep the rowdy element in check.

Comstock sighed. He knew Prudence would argue with his logic, but he had to get new saws and a planer mill in place, and a quiet situation was all he wanted until the equipment was installed and operational. Damn Matt Stryker. Comstock had promised to do what he could, but for a moment, he wondered if he should warn Nate Cahill. Maybe so. Maybe in the morning. He felt his way back to bed, but sleep eluded him. Matt Stryker didn't make idle threats. War was coming to Ponderosa.

When morning came, Comstock put off telling Cahill about Stryker's threat. He figured he could stand back and let Stryker and Cahill fight it out. Most likely, the conflict wouldn't involve the mill. Besides, whoever was in charge, Comstock had to find a way to work with them. He had a business to run. He couldn't afford to get involved in trivial turf wars or petty revenge plots. His decision made, Comstock took his time dressing. He chose fawn-colored trousers and an off-white linen shirt. He tied a maroon cravat at his throat and shrugged into an embroidered waistcoat. *Gold this morning,* he thought as he thrust a gold-plated watch into a vest pocket and draped his heavy beaten gold chain across his spare midriff. Nearly thirty-five and no sign of middle-age spread. Comstock felt proud of that.

His bottle-green topcoat with velvet collar made him look like exactly what he was — a business magnate and pillar of the community. Comstock picked up a light cane and stepped to the front door. 'Breakfast at Clark's,' he called, though the fragrance of chorizo and jalapenos came from the kitchen.

'*Sí patrón,*' replied Ramona, his housekeeper. She always prepared breakfast, though he ate at Clark's as often as he ate at home.

★ ★ ★

'Morning, Mr Comstock,' Dan Brady said. Comstock nodded to the deputy and barged on through the door to Clark's. Briefly, Dan wondered what was going on in Comstock's head. He looked awful preoccupied. Dan shifted his shotgun to the crook of his left arm and continued on down the boardwalk. The new rules said a badge had to be out on the boardwalk during daylight hours. That will show folks the law is serious, Cahill said, and Dan could see his point. Dan just didn't think he should do all the walking and badge displaying. Not that he minded seeing all the citizens of Ponderosa. He tipped his hat to Parson Hunt's wife as she entered the general store. He stuck his head in. 'How are things going, Mr Gardner?'

Gardner looked up from where he was measuring yard goods. 'Things are quiet, Dan. Hope they stay that way.'

'Reckon they will,' Dan said. 'Reckon they will.'

A murmur of voices down the boardwalk brought Dan's head out of the store. He turned to look down Main Street. Two riders came up the street abreast. People stopped to stare. The big man in a black duster with his hat pulled low over his face rode on the left. A wiry man on a long-legged dapple-gray built for speed rode beside him. The big man's hat put his face in the shadow, and his jaw showed dark growth that said he'd not shaved in a month or so. The smaller man's narrow brim hat hid his face not at all, but his frank open expression held a hint of humor that was belied by the sawed-off shotgun held like a lance on his thigh. 'Seen that black horse before,' a cowboy commented, 'Can't recall where.'

Dan Brady knew where. That black horse was Matt Stryker's Arabian. Dan scurried down the boardwalk ahead of the two riders and burst through the door to the marshal's office as the new arrivals reined in their mounts at the hitching rail.

'Marshal,' Dan said to Riddle, who sat as usual with his boots up on a pulled-out bottom drawer. 'Marshal, I think Matt Stryker's coming.'

'Matt Stryker?'

The door swung open and crashed

against the wall. A huge shape filled the doorway. 'I'll have the badge, Riddle,' a gravelly voice said.

'Like hell you will.' Tag Riddle scrambled to his feet. He pawed at the gun rig hanging at the side of his desk.

The man in black took three long strides into the room. His right arm snaked out to grab Riddle's shirt by the collar. Riddle lost his grip on the gun rig and it fell to the floor.

'You've dropped your tool, gunny,' the man rasped. He pulled Riddle around and planted a gloved right fist into the sham marshal's midriff. Riddle's breath exploded from his lungs. He doubled over, gasping, only to have a left fist crash into his jaw and send him sprawling. Riddle struggled to his hands and knees, crimson slobber drooling from his smashed lips. The man in black bashed a polished boot into Riddle's ribs.

'My God, man, you're killing me. Take the damned badge if you want it so bad.' Riddle fumbled at the marshal's badge pinned to his vest.

The big man stood spraddle-legged, his face hidden in the shadow of his hat's wide, down-turned brim.

At last Riddle managed to unpin the badge. He dropped it at the big man's feet. 'There's your stinking badge.'

He crawled for the door.

The man in black swept the badge up with the clawed fingers of his right hand. He pinned the badge to his black leather vest. 'Now Ponderosa's got some law,' he said. He sat in the marshal's chair and pushed the black hat to the back of his head.

Dan Brady gasped.

'What's the matter, son? Nate Cahill's handiwork take you aback somewhat?' Matt Stryker ran a hand over his scarred and misshapen face. 'Seems that I remember you were Braxton Webber's deputy. I see you still wear a star.'

'Yessir. This is all the job I got, Mister Stryker.'

Stryker smiled, but the scars pulled his lips in directions the smile never intended. The result was closer to a grimace. 'Does that mean you'd like to keep your badge?'

'Yes, sir. I'd like to get to be a bona fide lawman some day.'

Stryker raised an eyebrow. 'Did you hear him, Tom? We've got an idealist on our hands. What do you think? Shall we let him stay?'

Tom Hall had a smile on his open frank face. 'Don't see why not, Matt. We'll need all the help we can get.'

'You're right about that. All right, kid, keep your badge. What's your name again?'

'Daniel Brady, sir. Most people just call me Dan.'

'All right, Dan. I'm Matt Stryker — '

'I know that, sir.'

'And the little guy with the big shotgun's Tom Hall. He watches my back. I'm here to break Nat Cahill's hold on this town and my back's going to need a lot of watching.'

'He makes everybody pay,' Dan said.

Stryker nodded. He rummaged in the

desk drawer and came up with a ring of keys. He unlocked the guns and chose a long Winchester shotgun. 'Come on, Tom. We got work to do.' He shoved half a dozen shotgun shells in a vest pocket and loaded the shotgun as he strode out onto the boardwalk. Tom Hall checked his loads and left three steps behind and off to one side. No one said Dan had to stay in the office, so he followed Stryker. Something was about to happen, and Dan Brady wanted to be there when it did.

4

Tag Riddle crashed through the new batwing doors of Old Glory.

'Take care, Riddle,' said Nate Cahill, a half-sneer on his face. 'Those swinging doors cost more than two bits.'

'He's back!' Pink foam formed in the corners of Riddle's mouth. 'The goddam bastard's back, Nate.'

'What in hell are you blubbering about?'

'He was stark raving mad, boss, punching and kicking me. He woulda killed me, sure.'

'Who would have killed you? Where?'

'Over to the marshal's office.'

Cahill noticed the badge was missing. 'Where's your badge, Riddle?'

'He'd'a' killed me!'

'So what?'

'So I had to give him the badge, I had to. Or I'd be dead right now.'

'Ass. You gave away the law? Just

60

because you got busted in the teeth? I oughta kill you myself.'

Riddle backed away from Cahill until he hit the bar. He seemed spitted by Cahill's glare. 'B-b-boss. I couldn't do nothing else. I swear. I had to turn it over.'

Cahill upended his table. His glass and bottle of Turley's Mill crashed to the sawdust-covered floor. The glass broke, but the whiskey bottle was made of sterner stuff. It rolled around so Cahill had to step wide to avoid it as he stalked toward Tag Riddle. He pulled on doeskin gloves.

'Oh God, boss. I couldn't help it.' Riddle cowered against the bar.

'You gonna beat him, Nate?' Wynn Cahill stepped through the back door. 'Can I help?'

Cahill planted his feet and swung a huge roundhouse right that caught Riddle high on the cheekbone and sent him sliding down the bar. 'B-b-b-b-oss! Don't — '

Cahill's gloved left fist ploughed into Riddle's midriff just below his sternum.

He fell to his hands and knees, retching a thin stream of bile onto the dirty sawdust.

Wynn cajoled his brother. 'Come on, Nate. Let me have a turn.'

Cahill stood back. 'I don't want him dead, Wynn. And don't you cripple him either.'

Wynn put on a feral grin. 'You don't mind if he hurts though, right?'

'After what that ass did, he goddam ought to hurt. He let Matt Stryker take the marshal's badge away from him. Shit. That's going to cost us, and fart-face here needs to pay for it.'

Nate Cahill turned away from the blubbering Riddle. By the time he opened the door to his first-floor office, Tag Riddle's screams had begun in earnest.

★   ★   ★

Prudence Comstock looked up from her desk at the *Examiner* when the cowbell on the door clanged, announcing a visitor. The broad shoulders of the man nearly filled the doorway. He seemed familiar, but Prudence couldn't place him. The man removed his black hat as he came in, and Prudence couldn't suppress a gasp at the ruin of his face. Surely the grimace was supposed to be a smile. She quickly recovered her poise.

'How may I help you, sir?' she asked.

He grimaced again, the scars pulling his lips in unintended directions.

'I'm Matt Stryker,' he rasped, 'the new marshal of Ponderosa.'

Only then did Prudence notice the badge pinned to his vest. 'Marshal?'

'That's right. Ponderosa no longer needs to worry about the likes of Nate Cahill and his gang.'

Prudence couldn't take her eyes from the ruins of Stryker's face. His eyes twinkled back of the ridges of scars that surrounded them. 'I wondered if the *Examiner* did job work,' Stryker said. 'I'd like some notices printed.'

'Of course.' She retrieved a job form from the desk. 'Fill this in, please.'

Stryker took the form and fished a stub of pencil from his vest pocket. Prudence went back to the desk while Stryker scowled at the form, wrote, scratched out, then wrote again. At last he finished, and turned the job order over to Prudence. She reviewed the contents.

NOTICE

No one shall carry firearms north of Bog Creek. Drunk and disorderly men shall be jailed until sober.
Men who quarrel and fight shall be jailed and fined.
Horses shall be ridden or driven no faster than a trot.
No loitering.
No vagrancy.

Matt Stryker, Marshal

'I wonder if the law can enforce these, Mister Stryker.'
'Marshal Stryker, ma'am. Yes, we'll

enforce the rules.'

'But is it legal? Can you just make up rules like this?'

'Marshals do what is good for the town, miss, we make the rules.'

Prudence noticed Dan Brady standing near the open door. He seemed to be listening intently.

'Shouldn't the town council debate your rules, Mister Stryker? And shouldn't they decide if you're marshal?' she asked.

'Nate Cahill took over the marshal's office without a vote, Miss Comstock. Your brother — and the town, I might add — offered me the job of marshal. I was merely somewhat delayed in taking up the badge.' Stryker's hand strayed to his damaged face and a finger traced the scar that pulled his left eyelid askance. 'But now I'm here and Ponderosa will settle down and be civilized.' Stryker's voice went cold and Prudence felt a shiver crawl up her spine. 'I'll see to it,' the big marshal said, 'I purely will.'

A thousand retorts formed on Prudence Comstock's tongue . . . and died there as she looked into the cold hard ice-blue eyes of Matt Stryker.

'The job will be ready in the morning, Mister Stryker.' Prudence refused to call him marshal. He'd taken the badge by force, most likely beaten that Tag Riddle. She turned her back on Stryker and carried the job order back into the press room. She heard Stryker say 'Thank you, ma'am' as she shouldered her way through the swinging door.

Zack Everett stood before the type bins, setting the next issue of the *Examiner*. 'Job?' he asked.

Prudence nodded and held out the order. Everett wiped his hands almost clean of ink and lead and took the handwritten notice. His eyebrows shot up as he scanned the sheet. 'My, oh my. Things are going to get very interesting. Matt Stryker, eh? I heard he turned the marshal job down. Matt Stryker. He'll make the cowboys and bluebellies toe the line, if anyone can, but he's headed down a thorny row, mark my words.'

＊ ★ ★

Dan Brady raised his arm to halt the
Bar B Bar riders. 'You boys got to leave
your hoglegs here with me when you go
uptown,' he said.

'You by yourself, Brady?'

'Marshal Stryker says no sidearms
north of Bog Creek. So leave them
here.' Dan waved at the holding pen
behind him. 'Just unbuckle your gunbelts and I'll hang them on the top rail
of the corral until you get back.'

'Don't like going to town naked,
Brady. What do you say to that?'

Dan shifted to face the young
puncher. 'Willis, before you get your
back up, remember it's Matt Stryker
you're facing, not Dan Brady. All I got
is this shotgun and my old Dragoon.'

'Come on, fellas. We're just going
over to Gardner's store.' The blond
cowboy on the left unbuckled his rig.
'Here, Brady. Take it and be damned.'
He handed the Colt and rig over with a
smile.

67

'Thanks, Dandy. I owe you a beer.' Dan hung the gunbelt over the top pole while the rest of the riders followed Dandy's lead.

Seven gunbelts hung on the corral fence as the riders gigged their horses up the grade toward Corduroy Road. Dan heaved a sigh of relief. No way he could face down half a dozen men with two loads of buckshot. He pulled his Dragoon and added a shell so all six chambers were full. Marshal Stryker told him to collect all firearms at the bottom of the grade from Ponderosa down into Bogtown, and that's what he'd do. He was a little surprised to find the palms of his hands wet. He wiped them on the seat of his britches.

Dan collected nineteen rigs and four loose guns that he put on a square of canvas before trouble rode his way from the bowels of Bogtown. None of Cahill's gang was among the riders, but they all hung around Old Glory, and often did dirty work for Cahill. Dan eared the hammers back on the shotgun when he saw the bunch coming toward him from Bogtown. As they neared, the riders spread out. Now Dan could tell who they were. The leader wore a scar on his face, and they called him McGurty. Behind him, a youngster known as Kid Carl, then a rider who just went by Old Man, Quaid who'd almost lost his scalp fighting Indians, and Whistling Willy.

Dan's mouth went dry. These hard-cases were out to try the new marshal's rules. If they got by Dan, the rule of law might as well jump in the Comstock log pond. He wiped his palms on his britches again.

'That's far enough, McGurty,' Dan said. His voice cracked.

The scar-faced man grinned. 'Sure, deputy.' He reined his horse in facing Dan. Two riders kept on. Then they too reined in, and Dan faced a semi-circle of grinning hardcases.

'Just unbuckle your rigs and hand them down to me,' Dan said. He held the shotgun pointed more or less in

McGurty's direction.

'Deputy, I put my hat on first thing in the morning. And soon as I pull up my pants, I buckle on this here Peacemaker.' McGurty patted the Colt .45 holstered high on his right hip. 'I'd rather go without my pants than without my Peacemaker.'

Dan licked his lips. He couldn't point the shotgun at them all, so he left it on McGurty. 'Marshal's rules say no one goes into town wearing iron,' Dan said, trying to make his voice sound like he meant business.

'What'd you mean, 'Marshal's rules?' Last I knew, Tag Riddle was marshal of this burg. Ain't heard nothing different.'

'Matt Stryker's the marshal, McGurty, you know that.'

'Do I now? And where is this marshal. How come he's got a wet-back-of-the-ears kid deputy disarming us men?'

Dan wanted to wipe the trickle of sweat from his face, but knew any move on his part might start a shoot-out. 'Just hand over the hardware,' he said.

McGurty sneered at Dan. 'Suppose you take my gun away from me, deputy. Think you can do that?'

'I can blow you to Hell and gone, McGurty.' Brax Webber had always said to take out the leader of a gang first. Dan concentrated on the scar-faced man.

'You ain't got the guts, kid.' McGurty edged his horse closer and Dan backed off a step. The other men closed the semi-circle in around Dan, grinning like coyotes in a chicken coop.

'Defying the law can get you shot, McGurty. I'll do it, I swear I will.'

McGurty threw his head back and laughed while his hand reached for his nickel-plated Peacemaker.

'McGurty!' The gravelly roar came from the corner of the boardwalk. Stryker stood there with a Winchester at his cheek. He triggered the long gun as McGurty's Colt came out of its holster. The .44–70 slug took the gunman in the chest and slammed him

71

from his horse into a lifeless lump on the ground. The horse reared and whirled as the other riders clawed for their sidearms. Dan took three running steps toward Stryker and dropped behind a water barrel standing at the corner of the ketch pens. He triggered the right barrel of the shotgun as he disappeared. The buckshot went wide of the hardcase riders but a pellet grazed Old Man's paint horse, which reared and went to bucking. Kid Carl's Colt barked and water poured from a bullet hole in the water barrel. Tom Hall's shotgun bellowed from the south corner of the ketch pens and the Kid clutched a bloody forearm to his body and spurred his bay away toward Bogtown. Old Man couldn't get control of his crow-hopping paint, which left Whistling Willy and Quaid to face Dan, Tom Hall, and Marshal Stryker. Quaid snapped a shot at Dan that put another hole low in the water barrel. He whirled his horse as Stryker fired the Winchester. The marshal's shot went wide of its mark but burned a furrow across the top of Quaid's shoulder. The hardcase spurred his horse toward Bogtown and Whistling Willy followed. He'd not drawn a gun nor fired a shot.

'Let them go,' Stryker called.

McGurty's horse loped after the departing riders. Out in the long grass, Old Man finally got control of his paint. He'd dropped his six-gun to stay on the horse and now he held both hands high.

'Get over here,' Stryker shouted. He strode down the incline to meet the hardcase. 'Name?' Stryker demanded.

'Charles Jenkins, but everyone calls me Old Man.'

'Well, Old Man, we're the law in Ponderosa, and we mean to maintain the peace. You ride back to Bogtown and tell that to Nate Cahill. You got that?'

Old Man still held his hands at shoulder height.

'You can put your hands down,' Stryker said. 'I don't figure you're crazy enough to reach for iron right now.' He chuckled, but it sounded like gravel rattling.

Old Man gingerly lowered his hands. 'No disrespect, Marshal. We figured that green boy was the only one around. We were all-fired wrong about that.'

Stryker growled. 'That you did. Remember that lesson well. When you see one of us lawmen, there's another close by. We watch each other's backs.' Stryker waved at McGurty's body. 'And you tell Cahill to send someone out to pick up McGurty.'

'I'll do that, Marshal,' Old Man said.

'Git.'

Old Man spurred the paint and disappeared into the warrens of Bogtown.

'Think he'll leave town?' Dan came out from behind the leaking barrel.

'Or else,' said Tom Hall. His open honest-looking face seemed certain Old Man would choose atmospheres far away from Ponderosa.

'You hit Kid Carl with that shotgun,' Dan said. 'How come he never went down?'

Hall grinned. 'Rock salt. No need to shoot down more men that we have to.' He glanced at Stryker. 'Course, if Matt hadn't downed McGurty, you'd be laying there instead of him. Boy, you gotta learn when to stop talking and start shooting.' Hall smiled to take the sting from his words.

'You did good, Dan,' said Stryker. 'Here come the lollygawkers. Nothing people like to look at more than a dead body, except maybe a hanging.' Stryker's rasping voice carried a hint of bile.

As the gawkers gathered, three riders appeared from Bogtown, with a fourth horse on a lead rope.

'What'd he do to get shot?' someone asked.

'He drew a gun on Deputy Brady,' Stryker said. He faced the curious people. 'McGurty here reckoned he was bigger than the law,' he said. 'Had he respected the law and the rules the law prescribes, he'd be alive and well this very moment. Instead, he chose to defy an officer of the law — Deputy Brady — acting in the line of duty. Luckily, I was able to take care of McGurty before he shot the deputy.'

In the crowd of onlookers, Prudence Comstock scribbled on a pad of foolscap. She didn't look happy. Dan figured Prudence was about the prettiest woman on the whole Colorado Plateau, but she was almighty sharp with her words and independent with her thinking. She puzzled Dan more than a little.

The Bogtown riders stopped some distance away. One man gigged his mount a few steps closer. He kept both hands on the saddle horn so the lawmen could see his peaceful intentions.

'Marshal,' the man called. 'We come for McGurty, if it's all right with you.'

'You're the one called Breed then,' Stryker said.

'I am.'

'You'll do good to stay away from

Nate Cahill, son.'

Breed nodded. 'I hear you, Marshal, but I fork my own horses. McGurty?'

Stryker waved a hand. 'Take the body and be gone. Good riddance.'

Breed stood his ground. 'McGurty rode for the brand, Marshal, just like you. Sometimes doing a job can get a man killed.'

'Stay on the right side of the law, Breed, and you'll not end up like McGurty.'

'Begging your pardon, Marshal, but lead poisoning is what it is and where you stand ain't no protection. I've seen more than my share in the Nations. White Man's law ain't all it's cut out to be. Now, can we pick up McGurty?'

Stryker stepped aside. 'Give these men room,' he said.

Dan and Tom Hall backed up against the ketch pen fence and Stryker herded the onlookers a few feet back up the slope. Breed and the riders hefted McGurty's body and put it belly down on the extra horse.

Nate Cahill stood on the porch of Old Glory when Breed and the riders returned with McGurty's corpse draped over the saddle.

'What shall we do with the dead man?' Breed asked.

'Dump him on the trash pile for all I care,' Cahill said, 'but you'll probably want to get some men together to dig a hole for him in the cemetery.'

'He got any kin?'

'None that I know of. Mac wasn't the kind of man to spend a lot of time talking about home life. Just get him planted.'

'OK, boss.' Breed sat his horse, making no move to follow Cahill's orders.

'What do you want, Breed?'

'I'm thinking, boss. May not have been a good idea to let that white man live. He'll cause you a lot more grief before this is all over.'

'You just bury the body, Breed. Don't try to think.'

'White men make that mistake all the time.'

'Mistake?'

'Yeah. Just taking it for granted that a red man can't think. You watch out for that white man, boss.'

'I've got plans for this town, Breed, and Matt Stryker's not going to mess them up. After you've buried McGurty, keep the shovel handy so you can use it to bury Stryker.'

5

'Read the *Examiner*, Mr Brady?' Prudence Comstock pushed a freshly printed copy of Ponderosa's newspaper into Dan Brady's hands as he strode down the boardwalk toward Clark's Kitchen. He'd been up since four o'clock in the morning to take his turn at the night watch and he dearly wanted to get to Clark's for two or three cups of good coffee and Jimmie Clark's best Rancher's Breakfast. He could almost smell the bacon. But then, Prudence Comstock stopped the world for Dan Brady, and hunger could wait whenever he had a chance to talk to her.

'Morning, Miss Comstock. Turning cold of late. I'll have a copy of the paper, if you please. What's interesting today?'

'Five cents, Mister Brady. Don't forget to read the story on the front page about yesterday's murderous shooting. I wrote it.'

Dan paid and took the folded paper from Prudence and watched as she went up the boardwalk. Prudence seemed different this morning. She walked with a spring in her step that hadn't been there before. Dan put the paper under his arm and continued on to Clark's Kitchen.

The usual breakfast crowd filled Clark's. Jimmie Clark was one of the few who believed in showing a menu to his customers. The Rancher's Breakfast consisted of three eggs, four strips of hog belly bacon, potatoes fried with onions, and sourdough bread, toasted on both sides, and the meal always came with a pat of butter and a crock of high-country honey. Jimmie had his own hen house, but with cold weather coming on, the supply of eggs would dwindle as the hens gradually quit laying for the winter. Right now there was no egg problem, though, and Dan settled down in an empty seat to enjoy his. The meal came with the job, not out of Dan's pocket, and that made it taste even better.

Becky Clark passed Dan, her arms laden with plates of breakfast. 'The usual, Dan?' she said.

'Morning, Beck. Yeah. Eggs over easy.'

'You got it. Just give Jimmie a couple of minutes. I'll be right back.' Becky disappeared into the kitchen.

Dan opened the newspaper:

MAN HURLED INTO ETERNITY IN A MOMENT

Stormy as events sometimes get in Bogtown, nothing of that ilk ever occurred in Ponderosa until the events of yesterday. Following the unfortunate demise of Marshal Braxton Webber in Bogtown last fall, the town has been noted for its quietness and good order. It seems the quiet was but the calm that preceded the storm that burst upon us yesterday, although it burst not in Bogtown but upon the streets of Ponderosa as men who call themselves the law brought the thunder of firearms to the holding corrals on Corduroy Road near the Great Western and Santa Fe railway tracks in our good town.

Those known as cowboys have long been considered a frivolous element in Ponderosa and of late they kept their rambunctiousness to the other side of the creek. Recently, a new marshal presented himself to our town, taking the badge of authority he said by virtue of a calling by the town council, though no such calling can be determined by scrutinizing the minutes of town council meetings. This seemingly self-appointed law, in the form of Matthew Stryker and his so-called deputy Thomas B. Hall, yesterday shot down one Arthur McGurty who died on the spot of the gunshot wound he received.

When the new marshal took his

office, in the strictest sense of the word, he published a set of rules to which all men except the lawmen themselves were expected to adhere. Where others in Ponderosa are expected to go unarmed, the so-called law walk about with abbreviated cannons on their hips and double-barrelled engines of destruction in their hands.

Early yesterday Deputy Daniel Brady, the only one of the lawmen to have come by his badge in the recognized fashion, stood by the holding corrals by the side of Corduroy Road collecting the sidearms of men who were coming into Ponderosa. His presence caused some disaffection among the cow-boys but they all left their weapons with Deputy Brady and the morn-ing proceeded peacefully.

Soon thereafter calamity struck, which is best told in the words of W.R. Duncan who was an eyewit-ness from beginning to end. Mr

Duncan says, 'I was near the holding pens just south of the GW&SF tracks just after noon when I saw a group of men on horses crossing Bog Creek and riding up Corduroy Road. I recognized the man leading the procession as A.J. McGurty who rides for the Cooley Ranch during round-up season. Four men followed McGurty and I was able to make them out. They were Kid Carl, Old Man Jenkins, Whistling Willy, and a fellow they call Quaid. The men on horseback rode up to Deputy Dan Brady and formed a semi-circle around him so his back was to the corral. I could not hear what they were saying but the deputy looked concerned. McGurty put his hand on the butt of his six-shooter in a threatening manner and I saw Marshal Matthew Stryker step out from behind a building on Oak Street with a Winchester in his hands. When McGurty started to pull his six-shooter from its holster, the marshal shouted at him and when McGurty did not desist from pulling out his weapon, the marshal shot him through the chest. Then Tom Hall fired his shotgun and the deputy jumped behind a water barrel. A few shots were fired but no one else was killed, just McGurty.'

As the thunder of gunfire ripped through our peaceful community, concerned citizens dashed from their houses and places of work. They gathered at the spot of the shooting and observed Marshal Stryker standing over the dead body of Arthur McGurty. The marshal claimed the dead man would have killed Deputy Brady if he had not been shot, but no one knows the reality of the situation. In fact, it may be that the rules posted by Marshal Stryker are the true culprit in this murderous shooting. How long must our peaceful town kneel to a rule by force of arms?

Dan didn't read fast, but he read anything he could get his hands on. He liked the *Examiner* because he just about got everything in the paper read by the time a new edition came out. He'd finished the breakfast Jimmie Clark made for him and sipped at a third cup of coffee as he finished the *Examiner*'s front-page article. It told what happened, but somehow Matt Stryker looked in the wrong. Dan wondered if Prudence Comstock or whoever wrote the article had ever faced a drawn gun or been shot at for that matter. The tone of the article didn't sit well with Dan.

'More coffee, Dan?' Becky Clark held a big coffee pot in her capable right hand.

'Nah. Thanks anyway, Beck. I'd better mosey on back to the office.' Dan pushed his chair back and rescued his battered hat from the rack in the corner. 'You tell Jimmie the grub was first rate,' Dan said.

Becky smiled and waved a hand. 'See

ya tomorrow,' she said.

Dan tucked the paper under his arm and by habit touched the butt of the old Dragoon Colt he always wore. The old six-gun weighed nearly five pounds but Dan had never used anything else, not that he'd been in any gunfights or such. He stepped out onto the boardwalk and looked up and down Main Street. Maybe Prudence Comstock would still be passing out papers. He couldn't see her, so instead of walking directly back to the marshal's office where Main turned into Oak Street and intersected with Corduroy Road, he turned toward Gardner's general store and Doc Huntly's place just beyond. To the east of Ponderosa rose the White Mountains and to the north the land gradually flattened out into the Great Colorado Plateau. The Ponderosa spur line connected with the main GW&SF tracks just east of Holbrook, crossing the Little Colorado on a recently built trestle bridge. Dan crossed Main at the intersection with Ash Street and turned west on the boardwalk that fronted Doc Huntly's and the general store. The weather had become nippy and the leaves of the aspen turned bright yellow. Dan drew a deep breath. There was nothing like autumn in the high country. Soon people would start wearing mackinaws and sheepskin coats, and conversations on the boardwalk would be punctuated by puffs of white as breath froze in the clear crisp air. Dan smiled, the *Examiner* article forgotten for the moment.

★ ★ ★

Nate Cahill sat very still behind the big walnut desk in the office above Old Glory. 'Say that again, Mr Reeves,' he said.

'Like I told you, Mr Cahill, Fletcher Comstock's been collecting cash for about two years now. I know he's ordered a new Canadian buzzsaw and a planer mill and he's sending twenty thousand dollars to Holbrook on the train to deposit at Wells Fargo so he can pay for the machinery.' The man Cahill knew as Reeves stroked his full mustache.

'And why are you telling me about this?'

'Comstock is sure to put Marshal Stryker and that shotgunner of his on the train. I figure if you all were to invest in that twenty grand, Matt Stryker might end up at the bottom end of a shallow grave. He probably doesn't remember but a dozen years ago he tracked me down and turned me over to the sheriff. Funny. You can kill a man and no one hardly notices, but cut out a few dollars for yourself out of all those dollars some ranch owner like Willard Rogers over in Oklahoma has and they'll hire some gunhandy with a sharp eye to catch you and then they pen you up. Matt Stryker knew me by another name then, and I looked quite different, I'm told.'

Cahill's face held no expression. 'And how do you know of the shipment?'

'I've been the bookkeeper at Comstock Log and Lumber for nearly three years. Honest and trustworthy, I am. But I want Matt Stryker to get his, and I'd like to make a little traveling money.'

'How much?'

'Say . . . a thousand?'

'I'll give you five hundred now and five hundred when we get the jackpot.'

Reeves chewed his lip. 'All right.'

Cahill went to the Briggs safe in the corner of the office, dialled a combination, and opened the door. He pulled out a handful of double-eagles and counted off twenty-five, stacking them on the desk. He put the remainder back in the safe. He closed the safe door and twirled the dial. 'Five hundred, Reeves. If the twenty thousand is not on that train, I'll send my brother Wynn after you and you'll wish you'd stayed in Leavenworth or wherever they had you penned up.'

'It'll be there. I'll make sure you get word of when.' Reeves voice sounded confident, but his hand trembled as he accepted the downpayment from Nate Cahill.

After Reeves left, Cahill called Wynn and Morales to the office. 'Little bird told me Comstock will ship twenty thousand to Wells Fargo in Holbrook on the GW&SF before long. Wynn, you and Morales ride that train to Holbrook and see if you can figure out the best place to stop it and lighten its load by a sackful of double-eagles.'

'Costs a dollar to ride to Holbrook,' Wynn said. 'An' a dollar back.'

Cahill thumbed an eagle from his vest pocket and tossed it to Wynn. 'Make sure you watch the lay of the land when you're on that train. Don't want you carrying whiskey bottles along. Take Breed with you. His Injun eyes might see something you all miss.'

'All right, big brother. Ride to Holbrook it is. With Tom Stark marshalling and Commodore Perry wearing the county sheriff's badge, don't think we'll want to be too close to Holbrook when we stop the train.'

'We'll figure it out. Just you scout the land, and don't you let Stryker see you get on the train.'

* * *

Matt Stryker sat with his feet up on a pulled-out lower desk drawer. 'Been mighty quiet,' he said.

'Isn't that how you like it?' said Tom Hall.

'Too quiet. I can feel the storm coming.'

'You look for storms, sooner or later one's bound to come. Best be ready all the time, just in case.' Hall gave Stryker one of his slow smiles.

'I — ' Just as Stryker started so peak, a howl came from down Main Street.

'Whoooo-ee. Yippy Ki-Yi-Yay. Danny Brady's got my guns, but I'm still king of the mountain. Come on, whomso-ever is ready. Just see if you can knock me off.'

'Looks like the storm's in a whiskey

bottle,' Hall said.

Stryker dropped his feet to the floor, picked his rig from a peg on the wall, stood and walked out of the office, buckling the gunbelt around his hips as he went.

Dandy Brewer stood spraddle-legged in the middle of Main Street. 'Ho! Ho! Ho!' he crowed when Stryker emerged from the marshal's office. 'Ho! Ho! And what have we got here? The marshal arrives with — what did the newspaper say — an abbreviated cannon on his hip to arrest a poor unarmed cowpoke. Ho! Ho!'

Stryker strode down the boardwalk toward the drunken cowboy. 'You should have stayed in Bogtown, boy,' he said.

'Ho! Ho! Catch me if you can, Mister Marshal. I'm King of the Mountain and not ready to go to your jail.'

'I'm warning you, boy. The rules must be obeyed.'

'All us common folks got to toe the line. All you lawmen get to do as you please, eh?'

Stryker stopped almost within arm's reach of Dandy. 'Come on with me, boy. You can sleep it off on one of our cots.'

Dandy turned his back on Stryker and shouted. 'Hey everybody. The big gunslinging marshal of this burg wants to slap me in jail. Me, I ain't done nothing but yell a little.' Suddenly the cowboy didn't seem drunk. His eyes were clear and his steps steady.

'Dandy. I'm warning you. Come along.'

'Or what? Resisting an officer?'

'That's as good a charge as any.'

Dandy danced away. 'Don't think I'm as easy to catch as the ordinary drunk, Mister Marshal. Why don't you try?'

Stryker took a long, quick stride toward Dandy Brewer, drawing his Colt as he moved. Before the cowboy could react, Stryker buffaloed him above the ear with the Peacemaker. Dandy dropped to his knees and buried his head in his arms. Stryker clipped a handcuff over one wrist. 'Come along,' he said, heaving Dandy to his feet. Across the street,

95

Tom Hall released the hammers of his shotgun.

'Marshal Stryker, was there any reason to strike that young man with the barrel of your pistol? He was just funning.' Prudence Comstock stood on the boardwalk in front of the *Examiner* office, her arms akimbo.

'Maybe he'll learn not to fun with the law, Miss Comstock. His head's hard. His feelings are hurt more than his head.' Stryker tugged on the handcuffs. 'Come along,' he said. He led Dandy back up the street to the marshal's office and locked him into one of the two cells in the back. 'Let you out in the morning,' he said.

Dandy moaned. 'You nearly broke my head.'

'I've buffaloed enough rannies to know how hard to swing,' Stryker said. 'Now sleep it off. Whatever got your tail in a knot, it ain't worth the trouble you'll get.'

★　★　★

96

'He didn't have to do that,' Prudence Comstock grumbled to herself as the crowd melted away once the marshal hauled his prey inside.

'Lawmen are likely to see things by their own lights,' said a firm baritone voice next to her.

Prudence turned to find Breed leaning against the wall of the *Examiner* office. 'I believe people will abide by rules without force,' she said.

'Some will. Some won't. I don't like to see harm come to women or kids myself, but there's more than a few whiteman's rules that I could do just as well without.'

'Is that why you work for Nate Cahill?'

'Some, I guess. Met Nate in the Nations. I had to kill a man back there and Nate liked the way I did it. Said he'd heard of a nice town in the high country of Arizona, wanted to know if I'd ride with him. I had no other plans, so I rode along, did kinda what Nate told me to, but I take no guff from his brother Wynn. That man's got a crazy streak in him about as wide as the Little Colorado.'

'My, I didn't realize you were so articulate. I see Nate do things that are most likely against territorial law and maybe against federal. Do be careful, Mr — ?'

'Folks call me Breed.'

'I'd rather know your name.'

'My mother's people called me Stone. I left them before I could go on a spirit quest to earn my adult name. My father named me Seth, but that name don't fit well with my face.'

'And your family name?'

'My, you're a curious one.'

'Newspaper people ask questions.'

Breed laughed. 'The family name's no better than the given one — Graffunder. Can you see me answering to that? What's your name? Seth Graffunder.' Breed laughed again.

'I think Seth's a fine name, and so is Graffunder. I'll call you Seth, if you don't mind.'

Breed shrugged. He had a train to catch.

6

Nate Cahill faced his three men across the walnut desk in his office. 'How was the holiday to Holbrook?' The corners of his mouth turned down as if he scorned his own men.

Wynn Cahill hitched his butt around in the chair like he was not keen on reporting to his brother. 'Holiday? The only Holliday I know of is that crazy drunk gun-sharp gambler down to Tombstone. What do you mean, holiday?'

'Every day's a holiday to you, Wynn. I wouldn't expect you to know one if it bit your ass. Now tell me what you saw.'

Wynn's eyes narrowed. He leaned forward in his chair. 'That spur line misses every town between here and Holbrook,' he said. 'No stops going down the mountain, none at Pinetop or Lakeside, none at Show Low or Taylor,

99

a siding and water tower out on the west side of Snowflake where the train hardly slowed down, then nothing for twenty miles into Holbrook. We hit that train, and no one will know until it's past due in Holbrook, or, if you let it run on through, until it gets there.'

'But do we hit it in the mountains or on the flat?'

'Lots of cover between here and the cedar flats north of Show Low. Mostly open country from there on.'

'Wherebouts in the mountains, then?'

'There's a cut through a cinder cone east of Porter Mountain. It'd be easy to build a blockade there. Take them a while to undo the blockade after we left, too.'

Cahill scratched at his chin. What Wynn suggested seemed logical, but it was also the first thing a man would think of when looking to rob the GW&SF. He looked at Morales, then the Breed. Morales was not the thinking type. Maybe Breed was. 'Any ideas, Breed?'

'A couple.'

'Tell me.'

'There's a deep arroyo about seven miles from that siding west of Snowflake. It could hide a whole herd of horses and men, and probably runs all the way to Silver Creek Canyon south of Woodruff.'

'You know a lot about the country for someone that just got here.'

'I listen. I ask. It's good to know the lie of the land. A man of my color may have to take to the land without much warning.'

'How do we stop the train?'

'Pull a rail and leave it lying across the tracks just this side of the arroyo.'

'Hmmmmm. I'll think about it. Go have yourselves a drink.'

'Boss?'

'Yeah?'

Breed wiped his mouth with the heel of his hand. 'Ain't none of my concern, boss, but wouldn't it be better for you to let Comstock get his new machines for the sawmill?'

'Why?'

'Sawyers and loggers spend a bunch

101

of money at Old Glory. If Comstock goes broke, lots of people will find they don't have drinking money any more.'

'Fletcher Comstock sicced Matt Stryker on me, Breed. I gave him a lesson and sent him away, but now Stryker's back and it was Comstock who asked him to come and tame this town in the first place. For that, Comstock owes me, and he'll pay big time with the cash money that'll be on that train. Understand?'

'Like I said, boss, none of my business. Forget I asked.'

'OK, OK. Get off downstairs and have a drink, on the house.'

Cahill watched the men leave. What the Breed said about breaking Comstock made sense, but Comstock had to pay for all the trouble Stryker caused and twenty grand would go a long way toward settling the debt. He smiled. Then there was Prudence Comstock. She could pay some of the debt, too. Cahill's smile turned into a smirk.

Fletcher Comstock stuck his head into the marshal's office. 'Good morning, Marshal. Tom. Dan.'

'Morning, Fletcher,' Stryker replied. The other two nodded their greetings. 'What can we do for you?'

'Wonder if I could have a word with you, Matt?'

'Sure thing.' Stryker stood and reached for his gunbelt. 'Be right there.'

Comstock turned to walk down the boardwalk toward Clark's Kitchen. Stryker emerged from the marshal's office and lengthened his stride to catch up with Comstock. A moment later, Tom Hall came out into the sunshine and ambled across the street, his shotgun in the angle of his left arm. He followed Comstock and the marshal but on the opposite side of the street. His eyes flicked to every shadow and nook.

Clark's was empty when Comstock and Stryker walked in, as it usually was in the early afternoon. Becky came from the kitchen. 'Coffee?'

'That's hit the spot, Becky. Thanks. Sit down, Matt.'

Stryker sat back to the wall, facing the doorway. Comstock took a seat to his left, rather than sitting across from the marshal. Becky came in with two cups and a steaming pot of coffee. The two men said nothing as she poured the fragrant brew.

'Enjoy.' She again disappeared into the back.

'What is it, Fletcher?'

'I've got a favor to ask of you, Matt.'

'Ask away.'

'I've been collecting cash for some time now, and I've finally got enough to buy a new buzz-saw unit and a planer mill.'

'That's good.' Stryker blew at the coffee, then took a sip.

'But I need to send that cash to Wells Fargo in Holbrook so I can write bank drafts to pay for the machinery.'

'When?'

'The cash is in my safe. When would you be able to ride the train to guard it?'

'You want to send it on the train?'

'Fastest way.'

'Hmm.'

'You don't like the idea?'

Stryker scrubbed a finger at the scar beneath his eye. 'Be OK to make it look like you were sending it on the train . . . '

'Decoy?'

'We'll think of something. You just make sure everyone thinks the cash goes on that train.' Stryker took a deep swig of his coffee. 'Jimmie Clark knows how to brew that Arbuckle's,' he said.

'I hear you,' Comstock said, and sipped at his own brew.

'Watching over that little sister of yours must try your patience at times.'

'She's got her own mind.'

'That her mind behind the article in the *Examiner* on the McGurty thing?'

'I reckon.'

'She's not helping me tame this town.'

'I'm just her brother.'

'Sure would help if she'd quit her rabble-rousing. Cahill's enough trouble without having the whole town looking at us lawmen all white-eyed and skittish.'

'Matt, I learned a long time ago that when that girl gets her mind made up, she'll turn a stampede rather than change her ideas.' Comstock rubbed a hand across his face. 'Comes from growing up with no folks and a brother that pays no attention, I reckon.'

★   ★   ★

Clanton Reeves drew a big breath. 'Fletcher Comstock told me to get a strongbox for the machinery money, Mr Cahill. Said he was sending the cash to Wells Fargo in Holbrook on Thursday's train.'

Cahill sat up in his chair. 'That only gives us three more days to get ready,' he muttered.

'Er. About the remainder of my commission — '

'You'll get paid when we've got the money.'

'That's fine, Mr Cahill. I'm thinking

106

of leaving Ponderosa, maybe going to San Francisco.'

'You can trust me, Reeves. Just keep asking Wells Fargo there in the city. One day your commission will show up. You've got my promise.'

Reeves stared at the floor, then nodded. 'All right, Mr Cahill. I'll take you at your word.'

Cahill smiled, but it seemed to Reeves that too many teeth showed. He made up his mind right then that his destination would be El Paso and that he'd leave with the morning light. He excused himself and rushed away to buy a horse and pack his duffle.

'Wynn!' Cahill's voice came through the thin walls into Old Glory.

Wynn Cahill knocked back the rest of his whiskey and ambled to the back door. 'Gotta see what my big brother wants,' he said to no one. Across the room, Breed watched Wynn leave the saloon and heard his heavy boots clump up the stairs.

'I'm here, big brother,' Wynn said.

Cahill waved at a chair. 'Know Clanton Reeves?'

'That skinny drink of water that always dresses in checkered suits?'

'That's him.'

'Why?'

'I paid him five hundred for information. I got the information, and I think he's going to take a run. You keep an eye on him. If he rides out, you get my five hundred back.'

'Any way I want?'

'Any way you want. But be back before tomorrow night. We've got to set up for that train.'

Wynn grinned. 'I'll have your money by then, big brother,' he said.

'Good.'

When the gang saddled up to ride down country, Wynn handed Cahill a sack of coins. Cahill dug out a handful and handed the double eagles to Wynn. 'Commission,' he said.

Wynn grinned. 'Woulda been worth it just to hear that dude yell, and he did yell.' He pocketed the coins.

Each man rode his best mount and led a second horse. 'Wish we had fresh horses staked out,' Cahill said.

'Ain't gonna be no posse after us until it's too late,' Wynn said. 'Besides, no one will know who lifted the cash.'

'Still . . . '

'You worry too much, big brother.'

'Yeah, I reckon.'

The four men rode into the darkness west of Bogtown, paralleling Corduroy Road toward Camp Kinishba. They turned onto the freight road where it crossed Corduroy and set out for Holbrook at a slow canter. As they turned onto the freight road, Tom Hall stepped his long-legged gray out of the trees to watch the band of four disappear to the north.

★ ★ ★

Matt Stryker rode ahead of the wagon with a sawed-off Greener 10-gauge across his saddle-bow. Dan Brady sat on the high seat with the driver, holding a Colt revolving shotgun. Tom Hall followed the wagon with the scattergun he always carried cocked and ready.

At the headquarters of Comstock Log & Lumber Company, men loaded a heavy-looking box bound with iron bands and padlocked at each band. The wagon turned around and rumbled back down Main Street in front of the whole town. With Stryker standing watch and Hall guarding the turn-off, Brady and the driver hauled the box to the platform and loaded it into the baggage car where the mailman would guard it all the way to Holbrook.

'We'll be in the next car,' Stryker said, 'if and when you need help. You sit easy, Ralph, and keep that Colt of yours primed and loaded.'

'I will, Marshal.'

'If someone does hold up the train, though, don't you try to fight it out. Just let the owlhoots have the box and don't play the hero. A ton of double eagles ain't worth your life. Do you understand what I'm saying?'

'Yes, Marshal. I won't try to shoot it out with any owlhoots, but I won't make it easy for them either.'

'I'll say it again, Ralph. We don't want any dead heroes.' He stared at the mailman with hard blue eyes.

'I hear you, Marshal. If owlhoots come calling, I'll let them get the box.'

'Good.' Stryker turned on his heel and left the baggage car. Tom Hall stood at the entrance to the passenger car. It hooked directly to the coal tender and the baggage car came right after that. Then an enclosed freight car, followed by four flat cars loaded with lumber and the caboose. On the downhill run to Holbrook, the big steam engine should have no trouble with the load, Stryker thought. He walked down the track to the caboose, looked under the car, climbed the steps and opened the door. No one inside yet. He walked through the caboose and out the front, dropping down to the side of the tracks. He inspected each lumber-loaded flat car, then walked by

111

the closed freight car and the baggage car to the passenger car where Hall was waiting. 'All clear?'

'Seems that way.'

When the train pulled out of Ponderosa, Dan Brady saw the train off from the platform, then walked back to the marshal's office. Matt Stryker sat in the rear of the passenger car with his hat pulled low over his eyes. Six other people occupied the car; none sat together. Tom Hall was not among them.

Stryker didn't try to second-guess the train robbers. The train would start to slow long before it came to a stop at whatever barricade they set up. Besides, he wasn't there to prevent a robbery; he was a decoy. He slouched in the seat, hat low over his eyes. To the casual observer, he might well have been asleep, but Matt Stryker's nerves were stretched as tight as the strings of Abe Tenney's fiddle.

The train moved slowly down the mountain, taking more than two hours to reach the siding west of Snowflake, some thirty-five miles from Ponderosa. That left nearly thirty miles to Holbrook. Cahill's gang hadn't hit yet, but they would — Stryker had no doubts — they would.

When the train's brakes screeched and the engineer threw the gears into reverse and the big drivers strained against the tracks and began to shower sparks as they gradually started turning backwards, Stryker drew his Frontier Colt .44 and inserted a cartridge into the empty chamber that had been beneath the hammer. He wasn't there to fight Cahill. He just wanted to make sure the gang pulled off the hold-up.

The train came to a stop a good hundred yards south of Seven Mile Wash. A rail lay across the tracks. The train wouldn't get to Holbrook before the rail was replaced.

'Hey! What's going on?' One of the passengers, a drummer by his clothes, poked his head out a window. A six-gun crashed and the window exploded into shards. The drummer yelled and dropped to the floor between the seats. Stryker removed his hat and crawled to a window. He raised his head just far enough to see over the sill. Four men with flour sacks over their heads, holes cut to see through, sat their horses at the engine. The engineer and fireman stood by the steaming locomotive, hands in the air.

'Stand and you'll not get hurt,' the leader growled. The trainmen bobbed their heads.

'Take care of the freight car,' the leader commanded.

One of the men levered a shell into his Winchester .44–70. He walked his horse down the tracks until he was opposite the freight car. As the horse walked along the tracks, the man fired the Winchester into the side of the car about four feet above the floor. He levered and fired again. A horse screamed. He fired a third time and a fourth. In all, fifteen shots went through the wall of the freight car. The horse still screamed and struggled when the man rode back to the leader. 'Done,' he said.

The leader rode over to the baggage car. 'Hey! You in there. Throw out the strongbox and you'll live.'

The door edged open and the strongbox appeared in the opening.

'That's a good lad,' the leader said. 'You,' he waved at one of the men, 'get the box.'

The rider reached down and heaved the box up in front of him.

'OK. Let's go.' The four men rode down into the arroyo and headed east.

Stryker waited until the sound of their horses faded before getting to his feet and jumping to the ground. He ran to the freight car and rolled back the door. Saif stood pressed up against the back wall, trembling. Tom Hall's gray was down, a hole in its neck, and Tom lay spreadeagled on the floor, blood seeping from his chest.

* * *

'Stand back,' Cahill said. He aimed his Colt .45 at the point where the shackle

115

of the padlock went through the straps on the strongbox. Ordinarily he didn't even look at the loot from a job until the gang was completely in the clear. This time, the strongbox was big and clumsy. It would make riding much easier if they stuffed the coins or greenbacks or whatever was in the box into saddle-bags. Besides, they couldn't ride back into Bogtown with the strongbox in plain sight. Everyone would know who took the Comstock money then.

Cahill fired the pistol and the bullet clanged against the iron straps and the steel shackle of the padlock. He fired again, but the lock still refused to disintegrate.

'Shit.' Cahill smashed the lock with the butt of the six-gun. He might as well have been tickling it with a feather. 'Need a crowbar,' he said. 'Breed, ride into Snowflake. See if you can find us a crowbar.' He flipped Breed an eagle. 'That should cover it.'

Breed snagged the coin. 'Be back in a

couple of hours,' he said. His paint left a cloud of dust as it carried its rider south and a little west at a dead run.

Wynn Cahill dismounted and tied his horse to a nearby alligator juniper. He picked a likely sandstone outcropping and jacked the cartridges from his Winchester into his hat. He pulled a greasy rag from the near saddle-bag on his brown and sat down on the outcrop to clean the rifle.

Morales tied his horse to the same juniper, sat with his back to the tree, and pulled his hat down over his eyes. Breed would be back soon enough, and a man had to sleep when he got the chance.

Cahill holstered his Colt and picked up the strongbox. Heavy. He shook it. Whatever was inside clanked faintly. Coins. Double eagles, probably. At five coins to the hundred dollars, there would have to be something like a thousand double eagles to make up twenty grand. Of course, all the money didn't have to be in coins. Might be some in greenbacks. Cahill put the strongbox down. Nothing to do until Breed got back with a crowbar.

'Might as well grain the ponies,' Cahill said. 'Once we get the box open, we'll ride straight through to Bogtown.'

'Think I killed that horse?' Wynn wiped at the Winchester with the rag as he spoke. 'Sounded hurt some. The bullets I put into that car shoulda hit something. Only one horse in there? No telling. Wonder why Stryker didn't come out shooting? Don't seem like him to sit back and let someone take whatever he's guarding. That mailman was all fired cooperative, too. I was looking for a little more excitement.'

'Who cares about excitement,' Cahill said. 'We got the strongbox.'

'That we did. If we could just get it open.'

'Breed'll be along.'

Wynn nodded.

Morales snorted as he slept beneath his hat.

Almost two hours later by the watch

in Cahill's vest pocket Breed rode back with a five-foot crowbar across his saddle bow. 'Dollar and a half,' he said as he dismounted. He dug into his pocket and handed Cahill the remainder from the eagle.

'Honest of you,' Cahill said.

Breed showed a small smile.

'All right. Let's pry the locks off this box of cash.' Cahill jammed the blade end of the crowbar against a strap. Too tight for the blunt blade to slip under. He reversed the bar and hit the shackle-strap connection with the point. The box bounced out of the way.

'Can I try, boss?'

Cahill handed the crowbar to Breed. 'Have at it.'

Breed stuck the pointed end of the bar into the shackle of the padlock. 'Hold the box,' he said. Cahill and Wynn grabbed the strongbox. Breed walked the crowbar around the box, putting pressure on the shackle. Half-way around, the lock popped. The same technique broke the second lock, the third, and the fourth. Breed stabbed the crowbar into the ground.

'Let's have a look,' Cahill said. His voice trembled. He removed the strong-box lid. Old *Examiner* newspapers covered the contents of the box. Cahill grabbed a handful of paper and ripped it away.

'Shit! Shit! Shit!'

The box was full of rusty washers.

7

'Tom!' Stryker vaulted into the freight car.

'Ah. Ah. M-m-a-tt.' Tom Hall's voice was hardly a whisper. His face was white and covered with a sheen of perspiration. He groaned, but didn't move.

Stryker dug a clasp knife from his pocket, clawed it open, and cut Hall's shirt and long johns away from the wound. A deformed bullet had torn a large hole in Hall's chest. It bubbled and frothed with Hall's shallow breathing. Stryker shrugged off his mackinaw and ripped a sleeve from his flannel shirt. He folded the sleeve into a square, ripped off the other sleeve, cut it into strips, and tied the pad over Hall's wound. 'You lie still, old friend. We'll get you out of this.' He rolled the mackinaw into a pillow and placed it under Hall's head. 'Hang in there,' he said, and scrambled from the car.

'Fred! Fred!' Stryker ran down the tracks toward the engine.

The engineer poked his head around the cowcatcher. 'What's up, Marshal?'

'Those outlaws shot my partner. Get the steam up and back this train to Snowflake siding. There's a doctor in Snowflake, right?'

'Doc Heywood.'

'Move it, man!'

The engineer and the fireman clambered into the engine's cab.

Stryker ran back to the freight car. Hall still breathed, but the breathing was very shallow. His eyes were closed. Stryker checked the gray horse. Dead. He went to Saif. The Arabian still trembled.

'All right, all right,' Stryker said, soothing the stallion. He stroked the horse's nose, then ran his hands over the black's gleaming hide. He found one bullet burn across the top of Saif's hips, but otherwise the horse was

122

uninjured. Damn those Cahills! Killing a good horse like Tom Hall's gray for no good reason. God, but he hated people like that. The whistle blasted and the train clanked as the engine pushed the cars back against their couplings. Seven miles to Snowflake siding. Shouldn't take more than half an hour. Stryker sat down by Tom Hall and leaned his back against the side of the car.

The siding west of Snowflake was little more than a pair of tracks set west of the main line. The switch to put the train onto the siding was about two hundred yards north of the ketch pens and loading chute. The ketch pens were skinned aspen poles, brought down the mountain from Ponderosa on the train. Off to the east a line of willows marked Silver Creek and the roof of Shumway's mill showed red in the afternoon sun. In some parts of town, poplars were beginning to make themselves seen, and the sandstone walls of the new Snowflake Academy stood as yet with no rafters.

'Doc Heywood's place is on past the Academy,' said Fred Baxter, GW&SF engineer. 'You'll know it. The only place in town that looks like a little castle.'

Stryker tightened Saif's cinch and stepped aboard. 'Be back shortly,' he said.

'We'll water up while you're gone,' Baxter said.

Stryker gigged Saif with his rowel-less spurs and the Arabian was at a neck-stretched run in three steps.

Men working on the Academy building paused to watch Stryker go by. He'd slowed Saif to a gallop and the horse held his head high as he pounded down the wide street.

Stryker threw Saif's reins over the hitching post in front of Doc Heywood's little white castle. 'Stay, Saif,' he said, and strode to the front door. Pounding with a big fist, Stryker called for the doctor.

'All right. All right. Coming. Coming. No need to knock my house down.' A small wiry man with close-cropped white hair and a bushy black mustache opened the door. Before Stryker could say a word, the doctor spoke again. 'If you'd come to me when those wounds were fresh, I could have kept the scars from disfiguring your face like that. Now, there's not much I can do.' The doctor started to turn away.

'Not me, Doc. Got a man lung shot in a freight car at the siding. He's alive, was when I left anyway, can you come?'

'Help me harness my filly to the buckboard.'

In minutes, Doc Heywood and Matt Stryker went back past the Academy at a fast trot. Doc Heywood pulled the filly to a halt at the freight car, but he was too small to get into the car by himself. 'Give me a boost, young man,' he said to Stryker. Once in the car, with Stryker at his side, the doctor swiftly undid the crude bandage. Tom Hall twitched but didn't open his eyes. 'You did good, Stryker. Blood clotted on your bandage and stopped up the hole in this man's chest, but the clot was soft enough for air to escape when he filled his lungs. Good job. Good job. Many times it's best to leave these wounds to heal themselves, and they will heal if the bleeding stops.'

'What about the bullet?'

'It didn't carry a lot of pieces of shirt and other debris into the wound so we'll let it be. Do more damage poking around in there trying to find the bullet and haul it out.'

'You're the doctor. He's too good a man to get shot down blind.'

'Let's get him onto the buckboard.'

Stryker got some slats from the engineer and he and the fireman helped load Tom Hall onto Doc Heywood's buckboard.

The drive back to Heywood's castle went at a walk. Hall groaned every time the buckboard struck a stone or dropped into a rut. Doc and Stryker carried Hall into the dispensary at the castle. 'We'll put him on the hard table until I've worked on that hole,' Doc said. 'I can handle things from here.'

Stryker fished a double eagle from a pocket behind his gunbelt. 'Here, Doc. I'm not short of money, so do what's right for Tom. If I owe you more, I'll be around to settle with you. If he needs an undertaker, I'll pay for that, too. For a while, though, I'll be gone. The owlhoots that did this must be apprehended and made to pay.'

'You leave him with me, Marshal. Right now, he's got better than a fifty-fifty chance of pulling through.'

'My thanks, Doc. I'll be back.'

Stryker strode from the castle, mounted Saif, and struck for the railroad at a long canter. The engine had a full head of steam when he arrived.

'Run your black up the chute, Marshal, and we'll make tracks for Ponderosa,' said the engineer. In less than a quarter of an hour, the train sped up the tracks toward the White Mountains.

★ ★ ★

Dan Brady reined in the team of young geldings in front of Wells Fargo. He'd left Ponderosa as soon as the train pulled out, driving a light buggy with a heavy box on the floorboard, covered with a lap blanket. He'd seen no more than normal traffic on the freight road that ran from Holbrook through Camp Kinishba and on to Fort Apache. Now all he had to do was deliver the box to Wells Fargo, get a receipt, and drive back to Ponderosa.

'Morning,' Dan said to the teller. 'I brought a box here from Mr Comstock up to Ponderosa.'

'We've had a telegraph about your arrival, Mr Brady. Could you carry the box into the manager's office, please?' The teller opened the office door so Dan could go through.

'You'll be Deputy Dan Brady, then,' said the tall, balding man behind the desk. 'I'm Fenton Bowles, manager here at Wells Fargo in Holbrook.'

'Pleased to meet you, Mr Bowles. Could you count what's in this box and give me a receipt for it. I've got to get back up the mountain.'

'Certainly. James, count the proceeds in the box, please, and bring a receipt for Deputy Brady.'

'Yes, sir.'

'Now. May I offer you a cup of coffee, Deputy?'

'I'd admire one, Mr Bowles.'

The manager stuck his head out the door. 'Run over to Aunt Hattie's and get a pot of coffee, would you, Madge? Deputy Brady's been on the road a long time and needs some refreshment. Perhaps there's some apple pie left as well.'

'I won't be a moment, sir,' said a matronly voice.

Moments later, a large stately woman with her hair arranged neatly in a bun at the nape of her neck arrived with a coffee pot in one hand and a covered basket in the other. 'I'm Madge,' she said. 'I watch after Mr Bowles. I got some of Harriet's good coffee and a handsome wedge of her famous apple pie.'

Dan was nearly tongue-tied at Madge's

motherly air. 'Er, thank you, ma'am. I admire a good piece of apple pie . . . and good coffee, too. I surely do. Thank you very much, ma'am, I'm sure.'

Madge smiled. 'My boy would have been about your age if he hadn't caught diphtheria when he was a little tyke. I like to do for young men in his stead. You're very welcome, Deputy, very welcome indeed.'

Before Dan could finish the huge piece of apple pie Madge set before him, James the teller was back with a count of the box's contents. 'Mr Bowles, the box contains twelve thousand three hundred dollars in double eagle coins and seven thousand seven hundred in bills. The total is an even twenty thousand dollars.'

'My, My. A great deal of money,' said Bowles. 'Fletcher Comstock must trust you implicitly, Deputy. Still, I'm somewhat surprised at the amount.'

'Mr Comstock said he was buying a new buzz-saw unit and a whole planer mill,' Dan said.

'He's more than enough for that, I'd say,' said the manager, 'but it's safe here with Wells Fargo. Tell Mr Comstock that he's free to write a draft against his account any time he has the need.'

'I'll do that, Mr Bowles. Now, much obliged for the coffee and the pie, but I'd best be outta here. Long way back to Ponderosa.' Dan took the receipt for Comstock's money, bid Madge good-bye, and mounted the buckboard. He drove down River Street to Len Miller's livery stable where he bought the team a good bait of oats and rubbed them down. The horses were young and firey, and Dan figured they'd trot back up the mountain in good order. He'd rest them every hour or so along the road, but he dearly wanted to be in Ponderosa when things came to a head.

* * *

Nate Cahill and his men rode back into Bogtown in the dead of night. He didn't want people to notice his comings and goings. He didn't want to show the clouds on his face. He didn't want to pretend to be in good sorts, but come morning, he'd have to. 'Don't you boys go to drinking tonight,' Cahill said. 'And don't you talk about that train. Give me some time to figure out a way to get our share of that money outta Fletcher Comstock. Just give me some time.'

Cahill didn't sleep that night, but he dressed carefully in the morning, made sure to splash rose water on his face after shaving off his three-day beard, and pomaded his long curly hair. He inspected his reflection in the barroom mirror. Except for some puffiness about the eyes, he looked suave and debonair as anyone had a right to expect. Today he'd have breakfast at Clark's Kitchen. See where the chips fell.

'Bring my bay,' he said to no one in particular. Morales left through the back door. Old Glory now had a holding pen with a lean-to out back so horses could be unsaddled and gear could be kept out of the weather. A few minutes later Morales came in the front door. 'The bay he is out front, boss,' he said.

Cahill left his Peacemaker hanging on its peg in the office. There were rules against wearing sidearms in Ponderosa. He tucked a tiny derringer into a special clip up the loosely cut sleeve of his frock coat. Rules did not mean a man should not prepare to protect himself.

He strode from the saloon, placed his planter's hat squarely on his head, and mounted the frisky bay. He'd ridden the horse all the way from Oklahoma, and knew his habits. 'Come on, Red,' he said. 'Act your age.'

Becky Clark looked up from the table she was cleaning as Cahill entered. 'Good morning, Mr Cahill.' Becky's face was deadpan.

'And to you, Mrs Clark. May I eat breakfast here this morning?'

Becky nodded.

Cahill took a table in the corner near

the window. He watched the morning traffic move along Main Street. Prudence Comstock passed, probably on her way to the *Examiner*. A few minutes later, Fletcher Comstock came from the same direction, but turned into Clark's Kitchen. He scanned the room as he entered. His eyes stopped a moment when he noticed Cahill. With a slight nod in Cahill's direction, Comstock sat in the middle of the room. Becky came with Cahill's food. Now, with Comstock watching, Cahill lost much of his appetite. In fact, a stiff shot of Turley's Mill was what he needed. He broke a sourdough biscuit in two, daubed one end in the yolk of a sunny-side-up egg, and stuffed it into his mouth. The biscuit was almost too big to chew. Cahill took a gulp from his coffee cup. The brew softened the biscuit and he was able to chew and swallow.

Matt Stryker walked into the café and strode to Cahill's table. 'Join you?'

Cahill nodded at the chair opposite.

Stryker pulled it out and sat. He pushed his hat back on his head, baring his ruined face.

'Didn't figure you'd want to show that face around here, Stryker.'

'You tried your best to put a scare into me, Cahill. I don't scare worth a damn, and I don't stay run out of town.'

Cahill's breakfast sat on the plate, forgotten. His brown-eyed stare met Stryker's of icy blue.

'I have a little problem,' Stryker said. 'Four men with sacks over their heads stopped the GW&SF train to Holbrook three days ago. I couldn't see any faces, but the leader of that bunch sat his horse a lot like you. I figure they were after a box full of money sent by Fletcher Comstock to Wells Fargo. Thing was, as you know, the money wasn't on the train. Ordinarily, I wouldn't worry about looking for a gang that stole a bunch of rusty bits of iron, but one of that gang put shots into the freight car hitched on behind the baggage car. He killed a mighty good gray riding horse for no good reason, and a friend of mine is in Doc Heywood's castle over to Snowflake with a bullet in his lung. I'm telling you, Cahill. If Tom dies, I'm coming after you with both barrels. Even if he lives, you can count your days in Ponderosa on the fingers of your right hand. If I were you, I'd cash in on that saloon and try some part of the country with a more congenial atmosphere.'

Cahill snorted. 'I showed you what I think of bounty hunter town-tamers. I can do it again. You just step careful, Stryker. You got no shotgunner backing you now.' Cahill drank down his coffee, trying to look nonchalant.

Dan Brady pulled up in a buckboard drawn by tired horses. He tied them to the hitching post and came into Clark's. His eyes took in Cahill and Stryker, but he walked over to Fletcher Comstock. He pulled a piece of paper from his shirt pocket. 'Twenty grand in the Wells Fargo safe, Mr Comstock.

Here's the receipt. Mr Bowles says you can write drafts whenever you have a need.'

'Thank you, deputy.' Comstock took the receipt, unfolded it, nodded at its contents, then smiled at Nate Cahill. He looked back at Dan. 'Safe and sound, Dan. Much obliged.'

Dan nodded. 'I'll be at the office,' he said to Stryker as he turned to go.

'Take care of those colts,' Stryker said.

'I will. See you later.'

'So,' Stryker said to Cahill. 'All that money you thought to take sits down to Holbrook warming Wells Fargo's big old safe. Tom Stark's not a lawman to mess with, Cahill. If I were you, I'd try some other part of the country. I suggest you do.'

Cahill stood and put on his hat. 'I'll be in Ponderosa long enough to plant flowers on your grave, Stryker. You think you can throw me out? Go ahead and try.' He turned on his heel and left. A moment later the sound of hoofs said Cahill was returning to Bogtown.

Nate Cahill downed his third shot of Turley's Mill. The whiskey burned all the way down. 'Damn. Damn. Double damn.' He poured another shot.

'What you damning about, big brother?' Wynn shoved his glass over, intimating that Cahill should share the whiskey.

Cahill ignored him. 'Damn!' He tossed the shot. 'Our money's all down to Holbrook in the safe at Wells Fargo. Damn!'

Wynn waggled his glass at the whiskey bottle. Cahill continued to ignore the hint.

'This is my town,' Cahill said. 'I want my share of that money.'

'Get Comstock to write you a draft,' Wynn said, his eyes still on the Turley's Mill.

'That's an idea,' Cahill said. 'If I put a gun to his head, maybe he'd do that.'

'Seems to put some store in that feisty little sister of his,' Wynn said. 'I'd like a share of her while you're at it. I'll bet she'd yowl real good.'

'Wynn, if you were smart, you'd be scary. You don't hurt the girl, you just grab her and tell her brother to give us ten grand if he wants her to stay alive.'

8

Stryker buffaloed three drunken cowboys in as many days. Without Tom
Hall watching his back, he felt nervous
about letting things go. If he moved
quickly on minor offenses like drunk
and disorderly, maybe people would
think twice about doing something
more blatant or more vicious.

Prudence Comstock obviously didn't
approve of Stryker's methods. Every
issue of the *Examiner* carried an
editorial about the 'dictatorial lawmen
who have invaded our peaceful town'.

Fletcher Comstock was completely
happy with Matt Stryker. Not only did
he keep the rowdy element in check, he
had also figured out a neat ruse that
had put Comstock's earnings from the
sawmill safely into Wells Fargo's posses-
sion. And ever since Stryker had told
Nate Cahill off in Clark's Kitchen,

things in Bogtown were quiet as the moments of silence that come just before the whole powder keg blew sky high. Maybe things weren't so comfortable after all. Comstock climbed the stairs to the big room at the top of the hotel where the Ponderosa Club met every Thursday.

Although the club had twenty-three members, all prominent citizens, the steering committee consisted of five: Fletcher Comstock, Borg Larsen, Herbert Gardner, Melvin 'Slim' Welsh, and Xavier Gaspé. The other four were waiting when Comstock arrived.

'Sorry I'm late,' he said.

Gardner waved a hand. 'We've got things to discuss, Fletcher. Best we get to it.'

Comstock stalled. He opened the door in the belly of the Franklin stove and stoked it with a chunk of pine for quick flame and one of oak for long-lasting coals. The coffee pot on top of the stove breathed fragrant steam. Comstock got a porcelain cup from the

141

sideboard and poured it full of coffee. Only then did he take a seat. 'OK. What's the big problem?' he asked.

'Matt Stryker's getting out of hand, Fletcher. Ever since he came back without Tom Hall, he's been coming down hard.' Borg Larsen gulped at his coffee.

'Yeah. Too hard,' Gardner echoed. 'Do we really need a town-tamer, Fletcher? Nate Cahill has stayed in Bogtown. Tag Riddle's hightailed it out of town. Morales plays it close to the chest. No one can read the Breed. So the only one in that gang who's a problem is Wynn Cahill.'

A knock came at the door. 'Becky here. I brought a big plate of bear sign.'

'Enter and be damned,' called Slim Welsh, with a laugh. 'You know there's not a man in here but what wouldn't kill for a bite of good bear sign, and Jimmie makes the best.'

Becky opened the door and the smell of freshly cooked doughnuts invaded the room, making serious conversation

142

impossible for the moment.

Members of the steering committee of the Ponderosa Club sat back as Becky Clark placed the heaped plate of doughnuts in the center of the table. There wasn't a dry mouth in the house.

'How are you doing for coffee?' she asked.

''Bout half a pot, I'd say.' Herbert Gardner reached for a glazed dough-nut. 'We'll need more before this meeting's over with.'

'I'll bring more up.'

'Much obliged, Becky. Your coffee and Jimmie's doughnuts are the only things that make this company bear-able,' said Welsh. The group laughed.

'Be back in a moment,' Becky said. She poured everyone's cup full before leaving with the coffee pot.

'Don't know what this town would do without Jimmie and Becky. They keep us all alive. Now. About Matt Stryker.' Gardner took the subject back to the matter at hand.

'Seems to me,' Comstock said, 'that

the bunch of you were crying for salvation not more than a month ago. You screamed and moaned when you thought Nate Cahill had run Stryker out of town. And you crowed when he came back. Looks to me as though you all are a very hard bunch to please. As for me, I vote for letting Matt Stryker do his job. You leave him be and Nate Cahill and his ilk will find that the air here in Ponderosa doesn't agree with their kind at all. I say leave him be.'

'Fletcher talks sense,' said Gaspé. 'In Canada, we have such men as Stryker. Those mounted policemen make it possible for such as us to remain in business. My vote is with Fletcher . . . Also, I think Matthew Stryker is the very honest man. That to me is important.'

'So two of us want to leave Stryker be,' said Comstock. 'Herb, are you voting Stryker out?'

'The way he's been lately, I have to say yes. I want him out.'

'Me, too,' Larsen said. 'I have to vote with Herb.'

'So it's me and Xavier for and Herb and Borg against. Leaves you to break the tie, Slim. What do you say?'

Slim Welsh reached for another doughnut and took a big bite. With the sweet morsel in his mouth, he swigged at his coffee. 'Hmm,' he said, and took another bite.

'Coffee,' Becky called with a rap at the door.

'It's open,' Comstock said.

Becky filled all the cups again and sat the coffee pot on the Franklin. 'Those doughnuts are not disappearing very fast,' she said. 'Did I bring too many? I could always take some back. Cowboys are always asking for bear sign.'

'Leave them be, Becky,' said Gardner. 'We're having a discussion here.' He gave her an expectant look.

'Right,' she said. 'I'm gone. Someone drop by and tell me when you all are finished. I'll get the cups and stuff.' She opened the door. 'See you all later.'

'Two to two,' Welsh said.

Slim took a third doughnut, his brow

furrowed. When the doughnut was gone, his brow was still furrowed. 'I see both sides,' he said. 'I understand what Fletcher's saying, but I have to agree with Herb that Stryker's got himself a bit high-handed since Tom Hall got hurt. Hmm.'

'You know what happened before Stryker came, Slim. You, too, Herb. How much was it you were 'donating' to keep the cowboys out of your flour barrel?'

'Cahill's been very quiet,' Gardner said.

'Why?'

'Maybe he's learned his lesson.'

'Maybe he knows that if he steps out of line he'll have Matt Stryker down his throat.' Comstock took a fierce bite into a doughnut.

'Don't like the law scaring people,' Gardner said, 'and Stryker's got a face that would scare his own mother. Fletcher, he doesn't even try to talk to the cowboys now. He just whacks them over the head with that monstrous pistol he wears. It's gone too far, I say. Too far.'

Slim cleared his throat. 'All said and done, Herb, I'm going to have to stand with Fletcher on this. I don't think we're out of the woods yet. I wouldn't be surprised if Cahill and his men don't try some new angle before long, and I want Stryker to be here when it happens.'

'Majority says Stryker stays,' Comstock said, 'so he stays.'

★ ★ ★

Dan Brady looked up at the rap on the frame of the open door.

'May I come in, Deputy?' Prudence Comstock stood just outside on the boardwalk.

'Of course. What can I do for you?'

'I came to interview Marshal Stryker's prisoner,' she said. 'The constitution guarantees freedom of the press, you know.'

'Er, well. Come on in. No harm in your talking to a hung-over cowboy, I reckon.'

'Thank you, Deputy.' She stepped

primly into the office. Dan hastened to open the door to the rear cell area.

'I'll just leave the door open, Miss Prudence. Can't have you alone in there with a prisoner, even if there are bars between you and him.'

'As you wish, Deputy. May I at least have a chair?'

Dan dragged a high-backed chair in from the office. 'I'll be right in the other room if you need me, Miss Prudence,' he said.

She nodded, turned the chair to face the cell, and sat.

'Now,' she said to the cowboy on the bunk, 'suppose we start with your name and outfit?'

He lifted his head from his hands. 'Ma'am, you're an eyeful to look at, but my head's busted and I don't feel up to jawing with pretty girls at the moment.'

'That's exactly why I'm here, Mr —?'

'Name's Caleb. Caleb Rossiter. Most folks just call me Ross. My head hurts something awful, miss. Maybe you could come back some other time.'

'Just a few questions, Ross, as long as I'm already here.'

The cowboy lowered his head to his hands. The slump in his shoulders said he'd given up trying to talk sense to Prudence Comstock.

'How long will you be in jail, Ross?'

'I reckon the marshal will let me go come evening. He knows I got to be at the ranch tonight.'

'Why are you here?'

'I was acting up. Had one or two too many. Marshal plonked me on the head with his six-shooter.'

'Why would he need to hit you?'

'Reckon I was a bit rowdy.'

'But did he have to hit you with a gun?'

'Reckon that was the handiest tool he had.'

'You're not upset?'

'Marshal's got to keep the peace.'

'Goodness, man. He acts like a despot.'

'What's that?'

'A king. Someone who does only what pleases him and insists all others do likewise.'

149

'Marshal's not tough and the rannies will run over him roughshod. Gotta be tough.'

'Oh, my. Whose side are you on?'

'Marshal's fair, ma'am. I was wrong. I got no complaints.'

'Well. This interview certainly is getting me nowhere very quickly.'

'Just telling it like it is, ma'am. Just like it is.'

Clamping her mouth into a tight line, Prudence stood up so quickly that all her ringlets bounced. 'I'll leave you to contemplate your sore head, then, Mr Rossiter, and hope that Matt Stryker doesn't go too far.'

'He wouldn't do that,' Dan Brady said from the office. 'Marshal Stryker knows exactly what he is doing.'

★ ★ ★

Matt Stryker stood at the top of the Corduroy Road upgrade. Old Glory sat across the Bog Creek ford where Corduroy ran its way alongside the trickle of water in the creek bed until it reached the end of the swale. Stryker didn't know what to do. He knew good and well that the Cahill gang took the strongbox off the GW&SF train. There was no way a man could fake the way he rode a horse, and Stryker saw Cahill, Wynn, Morales, and the Breed in the way the four owlhoots sat in the saddle. Stryker came down hard on the rowdy cowboys, hoping to push Cahill into making a move. So far, nothing had happened. If anything, Cahill tended to stick to Old Glory, using Breed or Morales when he needed something from town. He showed no signs of leaving Ponderosa either. 'Damn!' Stryker said aloud.

'Are you daydreaming, Marshal?' Somehow Prudence Comstock had walked right up to Stryker without him noticing. He'd have to be more careful.

'Dreaming, Miss Comstock? What I'd like to do is dream myself right out of a job, but I don't see that happening any time soon.'

'Is that why you always hit young

men in the head with your pistol?'

'Doesn't matter if they're young, miss. Rowdies lose a lot of their steam after a gun barrel's been laid alongside their heads. Best attitude controller I know.'

Prudence Comstock took a step back, looking up into Stryker's face. 'If I could think of a way to accomplish it, Marshal, I'd put you out of a job post haste.'

'Why's that?'

'Ponderosa doesn't need a strongarm gunman to enforce its laws, Mr Stryker. Sternness has its place, I'll admit, but violence is completely unnecessary.'

'I've always found that a town tames quicker when you fight fire with fire.' Stryker shoved his hat back on his head. 'Take a good look at my face, Miss Comstock. See how it caves in around the cheekbones and eye sockets. Notice the scars. Look at how they pull my eyes out of kilter, how they make my mouth turn down, even when I try to smile. Listen to my voice rattle. You know who did all that to me, Miss Comstock? Nate Cahill. With doeskin gloves on his hands and lead bars in his fists. With half a dozen of his cowboy friends holding me while he smacked my face into the mess you see.'

'It's revenge, then?'

'Yes and no.'

Prudence raised an eyebrow. 'Yes and no?'

'I want the Cahill gang. Especially Nate and Wynn. Nate for what he did to me. Wynn for what I hear he did to others — Bart Sims, Brax Webber, Richie Brown, Tag Riddle and probably Clanton Reeves. Those men deserve to spend the rest of their lives in the Hell Hole at Yuma. If I'm to put them there, I must catch them out.'

'Mr Cahill seems to keep himself mostly to Old Glory, doesn't he?'

'He does. The day will come, I'll wager, when he shows his rattles. I know him for a snake, and I know he's poison. If you're smart, Miss Comstock, you'll stay as far away from Nate

153

and Wynn Cahill as you can get.'

'The *Examiner* is a newspaper, Marshal, and we can't print the news without information. Thus I must go where the line of information leads. Our readers deserve to know the reality of every situation our city faces.'

'I'm giving you fair warning. Stay away from Old Glory. Nate Cahill's a rattlesnake from Hell and your being a woman won't make no nevermind to him.'

'I'll do what I must, Marshal.'

Prudence turned in a whirl of skirts and walked back down the boardwalk with her head held high. In any other situation, Stryker would have applauded her grit. Now he only felt she was headed for trouble. 'Best shake the apple tree to see what falls out,' he said, talking to himself. He shoved his hands into the pockets of his mackinaw and strolled back to the marshal's office. Planning had to be done. A skunk had to be flushed from its hole.

'Turn Ross out,' Stryker said as he

entered the office. 'He's been in there long enough to clear his head.'

Dan pulled the ring of keys off its peg and went into the back room. Stryker laid the cowboy's hat and gun on the desk. Ross limped through the door.

'Take your hat, son,' Stryker said. 'And let your steam off the other side of Bog Creek from now on. I don't like to hit people over the head, and when the head's as hard as yours, it's likely to bend my barrel out of shape. You hear?'

Ross ducked his head. 'I hear you, Marshal. I hear you, but now and then a man's got to lay one on, and after a few of that rotgut they sell as whiskey, my sense of direction ain't too good. I'll try, Marshal, I'll try.' He picked up the hat and placed it gingerly on his head.

'Your gear in Bogtown?' Stryker asked.

'Old Glory. My plug's in the corral behind. Furniture's in the lean-to. Didn't bring nothing else except my gun and my pay, and I reckon the pay's gone.'

'Dan, you go with Ross to the top of the upgrade. Make sure he knows which way's to Bogtown. Give him his gun and let him go. Make sure the gun's empty.'

Dan Brady clapped his hat on. 'Come on, Ross,' he said. He picked up the cowboy's six-gun, rolled the cylinder to make sure it was empty, and stuffed the gun back in the worn leather holster. 'You should take better care of your short gun, Ross. You do and it'll save your life one day. You don't and it'll let you down when you need it most.'

'Boy, you're getting to be a philosopher, and you're dead right. Ross. You be careful. They serve poison at Old Glory. Not all of it in a bottle. You're too good a man to die young.'

Ross grinned. 'Ain't much of a choice around here where a man can sow what few wild oats he has. In Ponderosa, it's Old Glory or it's sitting on the porch in a rocking chair. Never was too hot with rocking chairs.'

Stryker barked a laugh. 'Get out of here, you footloose Jehu. Don't let me see you again except when you're dead sober. I'll tell you again. They serve up poison at Old Glory. Don't you die from it.'

'See you around, Marshal,' Ross said. He followed Dan out the door and went off toward Corduroy Road.

Stryker leaned back in his chair and put his foot up on an open lower drawer. Now, if he could just figure out a way to make Nate Cahill show his stripes.

* * *

Nate Cahill fumed. Damn. Twenty grand. His for the taking. Train from Ponderosa stopped perfectly. No problem getting the strongbox. No resistance . . . no resistance. Damn! That Clanton Reese must have let the cat out. How else would Stryker know? Damn! *Fletcher Comstock owes me money*, Cahill thought. *By God he owes me money.* But the money lay in the big safe at Wells Fargo in Holbrook. Cahill had no intention of going up against Wells Fargo. That was a good way to get federal law after you. No one wanted US Marshal Stomp Hale after them. He was like a damned bulldog. Worse than a hundred Strykers. Stryker thought he knew Cahill held up the train. He had no proof. Nothing he could do. Besides, what law got broke by taking a strongbox full of goldam iron washers? There had to be a way to get that money. Cahill slammed the flat of his hand against the top of his desk. He'd come up with a way. There had to be a good way . . . had to be.

'Boss?'

'Yeah, Breed. What do you want?'

'Tom Hall's not here, boss.'

'I know that.'

'No one's watching Stryker's back.'

'I know that, too.'

'Were I you, I'd be thinking of ways to get rid of Stryker.'

'I am.'

'You know, that girl at the *Examiner*

is no friend of Stryker's. You read what she's got to say?'

'What?' Cahill had better things to do with his time than read a rag like the *Examiner*.

'She's all het up about how he buffaloes drunk cowboys if they're a bit too rowdy.'

'So?'

'Maybe a few . . . well, more than a few, drunk cowboys would do away with his reputation. Once Stryker's gone, all you have to deal with is that kid, Dan Brady.'

Cahill brightened. 'Yeah. Stryker buffaloes a lot more cowboys. The girl paints him a bastard. Then the Ponderosa Club fires him. I like the sound of that.'

'I got work to do, boss. Just thought you'd like to remember about Tom Hall.' Breed let himself out. Cahill's smile was not a pretty thing to see.

9

Stryker bought a double-bitted axe at Gardner's Mercantile and carried it against his leg up the boardwalk and across Main Street to the marshal's office.

'Why the axe?' Dan asked.

'I'm going to shake the apple tree,' Stryker said. 'Maybe even cut it down. I'm going to need you on the shotgun. Grab the sawed-off 10-gauge and a handful of shells and come along.'

Dan jammed on his hat and took the short shotgun from the gun rack. He opened the drawer at the bottom of the rack to get the shells. 'Birdshot OK?' he asked.

'Fine. Make it two handfuls. You may have to make some noise.' Stryker added a sixth cartridge to the cylinder of his Frontier Colt .44. He picked up the axe. 'Don't you let anyone take a shot at me while I'm shaking the tree,' he said. 'Just pretend you're Tom Hall.'

'I'm ready,' Dan said, breaking the shotgun and shoving two shells into the double breech. The grim look on his face said he took Stryker's admonition seriously.

Stryker strode out of the marshal's office, across Main Street, and down Corduroy Road. Dan Brady followed three steps behind and off to the left. He tried to watch all the shadows like Tom Hall would, but wasn't sure he did it right.

The marshal took a long step across the trickle called Bog Creek and walked up to Old Glory. Dan was still three steps behind. He watched left toward Murdock's cribs, then right toward Comstock Dam. The dark shapes of tarpaper shacks dotted the swale to the tree line. Lights showed in two.

Old Glory's piano man played that new one called 'Chopsticks', then went into 'I'll Take You Home Again, Kathleen'. A rumble of male voices

161

came through the batwing doors as Stryker mounted the steps to the porch at the front of the saloon. Dan stayed on the wagon-rutted street, watching out for danger. Stryker switched the axe to his left hand and drew his Colt .44 with his right. As he pushed through the batwings, he fired three shots into the ceiling as fast as he could thumb back the Colt's hammer.

The room went still.

'Gentlemen,' Stryker said, 'word has come my way that says the games at Old Glory are weighted toward the house. I hear that the common sawyer or lumberjack or soldier or cowboy has the chance of an icicle in Hell of winning at the tables here. So I've come to inspect those games. Dan!'

'Here, Marshal.' Dan stepped through the batwings, shotgun ready.

'Keep that scattergun handy,' Stryker said. He waved to the men at the tables, then those at the bar. 'Stand over against the far wall, gentlemen. This won't take long.'

'Hey! What the hell's going on?' Wynn Cahill came barreling through the back door to face Stryker's gun.

'Hello, Wynn,' Stryker said. 'The law's inspecting Old Glory. Take your gun out with two fingers. That's a good boy. Put it on the bar. That's right. Now walk over here.' Stryker smiled. The effect was anything but pleasant.

Wynn stopped half a dozen feet from Stryker. 'What do you want, asshole?'

Stryker took a long step forward and hit Wynn across the face with his Colt. He reversed his swing and cracked the younger Cahill hard on the crown of his head with the gun. Wynn went down, unconscious.

'Don't do it, Morales.' Dan shifted the shotgun toward the Mexican, who left his gun in its holster. 'Put the gun on the bar,' he said. Morales hesitated, then complied.

Stryker turned to the barman. 'Jigger, pull out the shotgun. Careful.'

The barkeep took his Greener from beneath the counter.

163

'Pop it and take out the shells,' Stryker said.

Jigger did as he was told.

'Now lay it on the bar. That's a good man. Breed?'

'I'm here.' Breed stood against the back wall with his arms folded.

'Gun on the bar?'

'Rather not, Marshal. But I won't try for you unless you come after me.'

Stryker gave Breed a long look. 'OK. I'm here to check the games, not for a shoot-out. I figure Wynn's the only one crazy enough to go up against me and Dan. Just stand easy against that wall, men,' Stryker said to the crowd. 'I'll be finished shortly.'

Old Glory had three card tables and two for roulette. 'Scattergun on the crowd, if you please, Dan,' Stryker said. He walked to the nearest roulette table and felt beneath it, at the edge of the wheel. 'Just as I thought,' he said. 'Stopper. No one wins much at this table.' Stryker hefted the axe and brought it down on the roulette wheel.

The bit sank into the wheel, splitting it in two. Stryker chopped again, and again, until the wheel lay in shattered pieces.

Boots sounded on the outside stairs. Nate Cahill burst into the saloon. His string tie was undone and his pomaded hair had not been combed into submission. As he came through the door, he roared, 'Can't a man get a little sleep — ' He came up short, staring at Stryker's cocked pistol, the ruined roulette wheel, and Wynn stretched out on the floor. 'What — the — hell — is — going — on?'

'Inspection, Cahill. Can't have anyone running crooked games in Ponderosa,' Stryker said.

'I'll pay the fine,' Cahill said. 'Just get out of here.'

Stryker laughed. 'That would be too easy, Cahill.' He walked to the second roulette wheel and felt under the table. 'You really stack the deck, don't you, Cahill?' Stryker chopped the wheel and table to kindling. 'I reckon your card

games are rigged same as the wheels,'
Stryker said, 'but it does no good to
chop up card tables. Don't let me hear
of you cheating. Who's Ferguson Nye?'

A suave man in gray raised a hand.

'Nye. I hear cowboys lose regular at
your table. I'll not run you out of town
now, but don't let me hear of you
shaving cards again. Clear?'

The man in gray looked at Cahill,
then nodded. 'As you say, Marshal,' he
said.

Wynn Cahill groaned.

'I'm nearly through here,' Stryker
said. 'I do howsoever find the premises
somewhat risqué.' He thumbed back
the hammer of his Colt and shot the
plate glass mirror behind the bar. 'Get
one with no naked women on it,
Cahill,' he said, and shot again. The
mirror cascaded to the floor in shards.

'Inspection complete,' Stryker said.
'Let's go, Dan. The apple tree's been
shook.'

★ ★ ★

'Why didn't you plug the bastard?' Breed stood quietly while Cahill ranted. 'You were right there. You had your gun. You could have plugged Stryker dead to rights. Goddam but that pisses me off. Shee-it. First the money. Now my roulette games. And the bar mirror. You know how much that mirror cost? A hundred and forty dollars in Saint Loo, plus all I had to pay to get it here. Damn! I don't understand you a bit, Breed. Most men are loyal to the brand. You! You just stood there, gun and all. I don't get it.'

Breed looked Cahill in the eye. 'You invited me to ride with you, Cahill. I've come this far. You never asked me to be your bodyguard. You never said I was supposed to be loyal to you, whatever that means. I'll tell you, Cahill. I'm loyal to me. Stryker wasn't out for blood, he just wanted to make you mad. Sometimes an angry man will do things he wouldn't even think about with a cool head. If I were you, I'd eat the losses and let things go. Maybe even talk to that good-looking woman who writes for the *Examiner*. Tell her what a bastard Stryker is. Do more damage than a gunfight, I reckon.'

'Bullshit.' Cahill paced the room. 'I'm going to get that bastard. I beat him to within an inch of his life. Now he breaks up my saloon. I can get him again. Only this time I'll let Wynn slit his belly open and feed him his own guts for breakfast, I swear. I'll get that scar-faced monster. I will.'

Breed shook his head. 'I'll watch, boss, and stay out of your way if I can, but don't count on me bushwhacking Stryker or even ganging up on him for that matter. I like to keep things halfway fair.'

'Fair? Fair! Shee-it. Stryker comes strolling in here with a badge and an axe and a boy with a sawed-off scattergun, and you say 'fair'?'

'He asked for my gun. I said no. He let me keep it, knowing I'd use it if he made a move my way. He didn't.'

'You getting soft on Stryker?'

'No. Not hard, either. At the moment, I'm entirely neutral. Now, if you don't mind, I'd like to go take care of my horse.'

'You spend more time on that nag than he's worth.'

'Come the time, that horse may have to carry me far and fast. I want him ready.'

'Yeah. You've got a point. Get out of here. I've got to think of a way to get Stryker.'

'I'd leave him, boss.' Breed raised a finger to the brim of his hat. 'See you later,' he said.

Cahill sat back and stared out the window. Ponderosa pines waved needled branches in the soft breeze. Frost covered the needles on the pines most mornings, and ice rimmed the water in the hoofprints where horses and cattle crossed the Bog Creek ford. Damn. Somehow he had to get Stryker. Wynn still nursed the cracks put in his skull by Stryker's gun, but when he recovered, he'd be out for blood. Until then, maybe Breed's suggestion would be a good idea. Cahill retrieved his planter's hat from the tree and headed for Ponderosa, the first time since he'd stopped the GW&SF train. He wore a heavy wool coat made from a Navajo blanket and his trousers were denim, lined with flannel. The bite of the autumn wind coming off Old Baldy didn't bother Cahill a bit. He walked down Main Street on the south side, opposite the marshal's office, then crossed over to the *Examiner*. Prudence Comstock stood behind the counter when Cahill opened the door. Involuntarily she took a step back. Cahill smiled.

'Good afternoon, Miss Comstock. May I interest you in a cup of coffee at Clark's Kitchen? I have a story I think you'll want to hear.'

BADGE-CLAD BULLY SMASHES LOCAL PROPERTY

Local lawmen have once again shown their lack of respect for the business-men of our good town, marching into the saloon Old Glory and smashing two of that establishment's gaming tables. Marshal Matthew Stryker, accompanied by Deputy Daniel Brady, barged into Old Glory the night before last. Upon entering the establishment, Marshal Stryker fired three rounds into the ceiling, where the bullet holes can be observed to this day. The marshal then forced all patrons of the establishment to stand against the west wall. When Mr Wynn Cahill protested the marshal's intent, the lawman struck Mr Cahill in the head with his revolver twice, rendering Mr Cahill unconscious. The marshal then proceeded to smash the establishment's two roulette wheels. Mr Nate Cahill also protested the marshal's deportment, but was held at gunpoint. The marshal destroyed the plate glass mirror behind the establishment's bar, declaring its artwork 'offensive.' Mr Cahill estimates the damage caused by Marshal

Stryker's unjustified violence at approximately five hundred and thirty-three dollars. How long must the citizens of Ponderosa suffer under the yoke of this tyrannical lawman?

Dan Brady read the piece in the *Examiner* over breakfast. The facts were correct, but he figured Prudence Comstock fairly well disliked Marshal Stryker, and he wasn't sure why. That puzzled him. He sopped a piece of sourdough biscuit in the yolk of his egg and popped it in his mouth. Marshal Stryker had hit Nate Cahill in the money pouch, where it hurt worst. Dan didn't think Cahill's reaction would end with the nasty article in the *Examiner*.

Borg Larsen and Slim Welsh had their heads together at the corner table. They spoke in low voices, and Dan paid them no mind. Gradually, their voices got louder, and Dan couldn't help but listen.

'He's gone too far, Slim. Too far.' Borg shoveled a forkful of fried potatoes into his mouth. 'He buffaloes every cowboy on the streets, keeps the army out of town, and now he's gone to breaking up private property. You read the piece in the paper?'

Slim Welsh nodded and said something Dan couldn't hear.

'Maybe so. But there's limits,' Borg said. 'We get your vote, Slim, and we can throw him out. Get someone else. Or let Dan take over.' The men ignored Dan as if he wasn't even there.

Dan sat back to enjoy his after-breakfast coffee.

'I haven't changed my mind, Borg. Until Cahill is gone, we need Stryker. 'Nough said.'

'Damn it, Slim. What'll it take to get you to come around?'

'Borg, you can't fault a man for doing his job the best he sees fit. In my book, that's what Stryker's doing. I'll see you later. Got stock to feed.' Slim Welsh pushed his chair back and unraveled his lanky frame. 'Mighty fine grub, Becky,' he said, leaving a quarter on the table.

'Any time, Slim. Any time.' Becky swept his cup and saucer away and swiped the place clean with a wet towel.

'Time for me to go, too,' Dan said. He left a nickel on the table for Becky. The town paid for his meals. He caught up with Slim as he stepped out on the boardwalk. 'Sounds like some folks are unhappy with how Marshal Stryker runs Ponderosa,' Dan said, 'not that I was listening to you and Borg talk.'

Slim smiled. ''Lo, Dan. Nah, anyone could hear what Borg was saying. That man talks almighty loud.'

'He does at that. Anything I or the marshal can do?'

'Don't reckon. When you enforce the law, you gotta stand up. You don't, and the likes of Nate Cahill will make hoof-marks all the way up your backbone.'

Dan nodded. 'That's the way the marshal sees things, too.'

'I'd best get back to the Flying W,' Slim said. 'Borg wanted to see me, so I came in, but I've got stock to care for. If you ever get a day off, Dan, come on over. Nellie'd like to have you for supper, sure. Being without kids gets her lonely sometimes.'

'I'll do that, Slim. Thanks for the invite.'

Slim Welsh forked a paint gelding that stood tied to the hitching rail in front of Clark's Kitchen. Dan strolled up the boardwalk, greeting the people of Ponderosa as he went.

Matt Stryker had the *Examiner* spread on the desk when Dan returned. His face looked stormy enough to bring clouds and rain. He looked up as Dan came in. 'Wonder if this is the only apple we're going to get from shaking that tree?' he said, punching at Prudence's piece with a thick finger.

'You know better than me, Marshal, but I'd say not.'

'Probably not.'

'Slow day. No prisoners. No prospects.' Dan sat in one of the high-backed chairs.

Stryker stood and reached for his gun belt. 'Better take a round through town.

175

Folks feel better when they can see a star.' Then, as he got to the door, Stryker seemed to go very quiet. 'Another apple just fell out of the tree,' he said, nodding toward Main Street.

Three men rode down the street like they'd just come from Round Valley. Dan came over to stand by Stryker. 'Know them?' he asked.

'The man out front is King Rennick,' Stryker said. 'The youngster riding on the left is the rattlesnake they call Kid McQueen. The dark man with the shotgun goes by the name of Ace Tyler. When those men ride in, someone usually ends up dead.'

10

Prudence Comstock noticed the three hard men through the window of the *Examiner*. The leader, or at least the man riding in the lead, wore a short-brimmed hat above a clean-shaven lean face. His frock coat flared over the cantle of his saddle, but failed to hide the walnut handles of the revolvers thrust into a red sash around his narrow waist. He wore striped California britches tucked into tooled boots with spurs that had very small daisy rowels. A dandy, Prudence thought, but the hard look on the suave man's face disturbed her.

The youngster riding to the left of the lead man looked carefree and almost lazy. His gray Stetson sat on the back of his head allowing a curly forelock to hang over his eyes. Instead of a coat, he wore a cowhide vest over a heavy red-and-black checked flannel shirt, and his single sidearm rode high on his left hip, angled for a cross draw. His Levis covered worn boots and showed frayed hems at the bottom. His spurs were Mexican-style with rowels half again as big as silver dollars. His freckled face wore a lopsided grin and his blue eyes sparkled just for the hell of it.

The small man on the right reminded Prudence of Tom Hall. Maybe it was the shotgun. Or perhaps the long-legged gray mare the man rode. He didn't look like Hall, who always kept himself neat. This man obviously hadn't shaved for several days. His coat was greasy buckskin and his trousers showed fraying at the knees. The shotgun shone as if it had been polished like a gem, and the gun belt at the man's waist looked well cared for.

Prudence stepped out of the *Examiner* office after the three men rode past. Marshal Stryker stood at the edge of the boardwalk, facing the riders.

'Hello, King,' Stryker said.

'Matthew,' the leader said, drawing his horse to a halt.

'Staying long? Or just riding through?'

'Shouldn't be here long, Matthew. You might say we're riding through.'

'We have a rule in Ponderosa, King. No firearms in town. You've just ridden in and didn't know, but next time I see you, you should be without the Remingtons.'

'And if I'm not?'

'I'll let you keep me company from behind our cell bars, King.'

'You think you could jail me?'

'Yes.'

The two men stared at each other for a long moment.

'Maybe so,' King Rennick said. 'Maybe so.' He clucked to his bay, which walked on down Main.

'King,' Stryker said. 'If you've come after me, make it out in the open. Bushwhacking isn't your style. And I've heard the Kid and Ace are honorable men.'

King Rennick chuckled. 'If you ever

take a bullet of mine, Matthew, you'll see it coming, you'll truly see it.'

'Just remember to leave the guns at home next time you come to Ponderosa,' Stryker said.

King raised a finger to his hat brim. 'See you around, Marshal,' emphasizing the 'marshal.' The three riders took Corduroy Road down the grade and across the Bog Creek ford. They stopped in front of Old Glory, dismounted, and went in.

Back in the *Examiner* office, Prudence thought about what she had heard. Could it be that those three men had come to Ponderosa to kill Marshal Stryker? *Serves him right*, she thought, *his high-handed ways have brought this down upon him*. If those in authority lorded it over everyone else, then the oppressed have every right to rebel. That was what had happened at the Boston Tea Party. That's what happened at Fort Sumner. That's what happened every time. Still, the three men bothered her. They looked like gunfighters. Mercenaries. Men whose fighting ability was for sale, to be bought and paid for. Shouldn't people fight their own wars? A shiver coursed through her body. Someone had hired those men to kill.

★　★　★

'Glad to see you men in Ponderosa,' Nate Cahill said. 'Have a seat. Drink?'

'Never touch the stuff,' King Rennick said, 'but the Kid likes a shot now and again. Ace does his drinking by the bottle, but he's going to wait until this little job is done. Now, let's see the color of your money.'

Wynn Cahill growled.

'Take it easy, Wynn. That's what I like about King. He's all business. No chance of feelings getting in the way. Right, King?'

'Not a chance.'

Cahill opened the safe in the corner of the room and pulled out a heavy sack. 'Here. One thousand in double

181

eagles just for taking on the job. When Matt Stryker is dead, I'll match that with another thousand before you leave town.'

King Rennick opened the leather pouch and reached in for a handful of coins. He bit one. 'Genuine stuff,' he said, passing a coin to Kid McQueen and another to Ace Tyler.

'Now, we need to coordinate our actions,' Cahill said. 'I've got a little plan to earn some more money, and it will go a lot smoother if Stryker's out of the way. When do you plan on doing the job?'

'Stryker seen us riding in — not that we were trying to sneak by — but he seen us, and he knows we're after him. He'll be on the look-out.'

'Ought to be some place you could waylay him.'

'That ain't my way of doing things, Cahill. I can take Matthew Stryker, and I'll do it in broad daylight. I just need to get the lay of the town and some idea of Stryker's habits. Give me three days.'

King Rennick and his two men took rooms in the Comstock Hotel, and when they ate at Clark's Kitchen they wore no guns in sight. King spent the next day walking the streets of Ponderosa and going around the Comstock Sawmill. He watched the pond rats manuever big ponderosa pine logs to the lift chain where gears from the steam engine caused the link chains to tighten over big cogwheels and lift the logs out of the pond and onto a slide that led to the buzz-saw carriage. He stood just outside where he could see the buzz-saw carriage and its rider taking two-inch fletches off the logs. King watched the sawmill work intently but saw no advantage there for him and his men. He spent the afternoon at Old Glory, talking to the soldiers and cowboys, and later, the sawyers who gathered there to drink arsenic-laced whiskey and gamble away their meagre earnings at the poker tables or hold hands with some of the girls sent over from Bucktooth Alice Murdock's place.

The first day, King didn't make up his mind. He'd take the day to look the town over before he sent his challenge to Matt Stryker.

While King and Ace and the Kid spent the evening at Old Glory, Matt Stryker walked the town and sat in the marshal's office while Dan made his rounds. The autumn air nipped exposed flesh at night and left rosettes of frost on the grass by morning. Ponderosa sat in the foothills of the White Mountains at the south edge of the Great Colorado Plateau, more than 7,000 feet above sea level. Winter came early, and when the log pond froze up hard in December, the sawmill had to shut down, and sawyers and pond rats and machinists had to exist somehow on meagre savings until spring thaw.

If rumor had it right, this year's winter might hold jobs for some of the crew. Backroom gossip said Fletcher Comstock would expand the mill with a new buzz-saw unit and build a whole new planer mill. That should mean work for many if not all of those laid off for the season.

Marshaling, however, was full-time work with no accounting for the seasons. Stryker hoped Comstock would get the construction started soon. Men with jobs were less likely to get in trouble than those with time on their hands. He leaned back in the desk chair and put his feet on a pulled-out drawer. He'd seen King Rennick casing the town. No use worrying about it. What would come would come.

Stryker caught the sound of a horse coming down Main from Corduroy. He thought little of it until the horse halted in front of the office. Stryker took his feet off the drawer. Footsteps sounded on the boardwalk and a rap came on the door.

'It's open,' Stryker called.

The door opened and Tom Hall stood there with a hand on the frame. 'Got a place where a wounded man could sit down?'

'Tom! For God's sake, man. You

should be in bed. What in hell are you doing here? Come in. Take a chair.'

Tom walked slowly across the room to sit in a high-backed chair. 'Kept thinking about that train robbery,' he said. 'Figured Cahill wouldn't be happy with a box full of washers. He'll try something else, Matt. He'll want to get back at you for outsmarting him, and he'll take another stab at Fletcher Comstock's money, somehow. You're going to need more back-up than Dan Brady can give you, good man though he is. So I'm here. I'm not all the way healed, but I can pull a trigger.'

'King Rennick's here, Tom.'

'No shit. Cahill's getting serious about things, then.'

'He is. Talked to Rennick. He's got a certain kind of pride. Don't think he'll try to shoot me blind.'

'When did he get here?'

'Yesterday.'

'It'll be tomorrow or the next day, then. Any idea where?'

'He's been looking the town over,'

Stryker said. 'Don't know what's in his mind, but I can't see any place for an open gunfight other than the GW&SF ketch pens.'

'Figure he'll call you out?'

'I reckon.'

Hall chewed at his lower lip. 'He by himself?'

'With Kid McQueen and Ace Tyler,' Stryker said.

'They'll come all spread out. That Tyler's a good man with a scattergun.'

'We'll just have to meet them.'

Tom smiled. 'You and Dan will. I'll just take my time and watch your back.'

★   ★   ★

Dan Brady stopped by Clark's Kitchen for a cup or two of coffee as he made the rounds of Main, Corduroy, Ash and Oak Streets. With the nightlife all across the ford in Bogtown, Ponderosa was quiet. When he finished the coffee, he'd take a turn through Bogtown. Old Glory was the only big drinkery there, but Charlie's Place, a joint with a plank on two barrels for a bar and no chairs, and Knute's Bar, which dipped drinks directly from a barrel of whiskey at five cents a shot, gave those with fewer coins in their jeans somewhere to take the edge off their sorrows.

Dan was only halfway through the first cup of coffee when Prudence Comstock came in.

'May I sit with you, Deputy?' she asked.

Dan nearly swallowed his tongue. He'd almost give his right arm to have Prudence Comstock sit with him. His neck flared crimson, but he managed to say, 'Why, sure,' without his voice trembling too much.

'Coffee for me, too, please,' Prudence said, as Becky poked her head in from the kitchen.

'Be right there,' she said.

'Quiet tonight, Deputy?'

She's just making conversation, Dan thought. 'Yes, ma'am,' he said. He gulped at his coffee.

'If only it were quiet every night,' she said, her voice sounding wistful.

'Marshal Stryker will soon have this town tamed,' Dan said.

'By hitting drunken men in the head with his pistol?'

'Miss Comstock, I don't want to argue with you. The marshal does his job as he sees is right. I second him.'

'I apologize, Deputy. I really came in to ask you a question. Would you deign to answer a question for me?'

Dan didn't know what deign meant, so he took another gulp of coffee. 'I suppose I could answer,' he said, careful to keep his tone of voice flat and noncommittal.

'Fine. Did you see three men ride in yesterday?'

'I did.'

'Who is King? Who are they?'

'Killers.'

Prudence searched Dan's face. 'Honestly? Killers?'

'The leader is King Rennick. The youngster is Kid McQueen. The man with the shotgun is Ace Tyler. You're in the newspaper business. You've heard about King Rennick and the Nueces War? Well, since then, Rennick, the Kid, or Ace have shot it out in Telluride, Alder Gulch, Gila Bend, and I don't know how many other places. So far, the other people have all ended up dead. King's bunch stays alive and seems to be pretty flush.

'Why would they come to Ponderosa?'

'Why do you think?'

'Has someone hired them? Who? To kill whom?'

Dan's voice grew stronger and took on an edge. 'Only one man stands to gain something if another dies — Nate Cahill wants Matt Stryker dead. I can't prove it, but I'd say Cahill hired Rennick's bunch to shoot it out with Matt Stryker — and me.'

Prudence's eyes widened. 'You?'

Dan nodded. 'I wear a badge. I back the marshal. They kill him, they gotta kill me, too.'

Prudence Comstock ate supper at Clark's Kitchen and lingered over her meal of boiled beef, potatoes, and carrots. Autumn was apple season for the few fruit trees in Ponderosa, and Jimmie created the best deep-dish apple pie Prudence had ever tasted. She dribbled rich cream over the steaming desert, then had Becky refill her cup of coffee. She spent the better part of an hour savoring the pie, and left the restaurant just before its nine o'clock closing hour.

''Night, Becky,' she called, leaving fifty cents for the meal. She shrugged into a woolen overcoat and tied a scarf over her hair and ears. She closed the door behind her and turned right toward the office of the *Examiner*. As she passed the alleyway between the Comstock Hotel and Clark's Kitchen, hard hands grasped her arm and jerked her into the gloom of the alley. Before she could more than squeak in surprise, a thick hand covered her mouth and rough fingers pinched her nose. She struggled to breathe. *Don't kill me. I don't want to die. Don't kill me*, she screamed, but could not make a sound. Her heart raced and she struggled harder to breathe.

'Shut up, bitch, and you won't get hurt,' a voice growled in her ear. Frantically, she nodded her head, her eyes wide and showing white all around. The hand loosened slightly and she was able to take a breath. She sucked a huge lungful of air, and the hand clamped down again. 'Don't you even think of making noise. Your life's not worth shit,' the voice growled again. 'Give me her scarf,' he said to someone else. She realized two pairs of hands held her. Who? She strained to see her assailants but the alleyway was too dark. Hands forced a wad of cloth into her mouth, then tied the gag tight behind her neck. 'Blindfold,' the voice said, and her eyes were covered with something and tied tightly in place. *Oh,*

God. Please. I don't want to die. Her thoughts tumbled one over the other.

The men — she thought of her assailants as men — pulled her farther into the alleyway. Then she smelled horses, the scent of sweat and droppings and warm horsehide.

'We're going to put you on a horse. You can ride astride or belly over the saddle, it makes no nevermind to me. What'll it be? Over the saddle? Astride?'

Prudence nodded vigorously at the last suggestion.

'Here's the stirrup.' Rough hands took her hand and brought it into contact with the stirrup. 'Use your left foot.' She nodded again and lifted her foot to the stirrup. Hands guided her grip to the saddle horn, and pushed on her butt as she mounted the horse.

'You going to sit, or do I have to tie you to the saddle?' A man looped what felt like a piggin string around her wrists and tied her hands to the saddle horn. 'Sit easy. Don't try anything.'

She heard two others mount, then

the horses started off at a walk. Prudence had no way of knowing where the men were taking her or what they would do with her when they got where they were going. Her mind sifted through the possibilities. She didn't like any of them.

Prudence felt like they rode for hours. In reality it was probably not more than half an hour. The little cavalcade stopped, and Prudence heard a gate complain as it opened. Hands undid the piggin string and pulled her from the saddle.

The men dragged her along and finally shoved her through a door. She stumbled across the uneven dirt floor and fell against some bulging sacks. The place smelled of oat chaff and oiled leather. Tack room? Granary? She shivered in the cold.

'Don't want you hurting yourself,' the gruff voice said. Hands guided her to a pile of gunnysacks full of grain and seated her on one. She heard the sound of tearing cloth, then someone tied her hands tightly behind her back with a strip of cloth that felt like canvas. The man also tied her feet at the ankles. Prudence could move neither hands nor feet; they were tied securely. Furthermore, the gag in her mouth prevented her from using her teeth to work on the strips that bound her.

'That should hold her,' the gravelly voice said. 'But you stay on guard outside, just in case.'

Someone threw a wool blanket that smelled of horse over her shoulders. Footsteps went away. The door closed. A hasp and lock clicked. Prudence was alone.

For several moments she tried to pant for breath, but the gag forced her to draw deeply through her nose. The effort helped calm her, and she was eventually able to sit quietly and think about her situation. The men had handled her roughly, both with their hands and with their words, but if they were going to kill her, why wait? If they were going to rape her, why wait?

Something else was happening. She worked at her hands and feet, but there was no give in the bindings. The cold made her shiver. The gag stretched the edges of her mouth and forced dry and bulky wool against her tongue. She toppled over and lay on the sacks. She rubbed her head against the rough burlap. Her hair slipped upwards, taking the blindfold with it. Now she could open her eyes. Black. Completely black. She scraped the side of her face against the sack, trying to loosen the gag. At first there was no give, but as with the blindfold, the thugs had tied the gag over her hair, and it was slippery enough to allow the gag to move up and down. Half the night, it seemed, she worked at the gag, and finally it fell down around her neck. She gulped for air. It was full of dust from gunnysacks and loose oats, but it tasted delicious to Prudence. Now, if anyone happened by, she could scream for help.

11

Matt Stryker ate breakfast at Clark's Kitchen shortly after it opened at six o'clock. Today was no exception. He had the usual: three eggs sunny-side-up, a rasher of bacon fried just short of crisp, a mound of fried potatoes almost black with cracked pepper, four slices of well-toasted and buttered sourdough bread, and a large mug of Becky's coffee, regularly refilled. He took his time eating, greeting the regular customers as they came in, but engaging in no extended conversations. He'd almost finished when King Rennick entered.

'Good morning, Matthew,' King said. 'Looks to be a bright day in the making.'

'King. Are you about ready to leave town?'

'One small matter to settle first, Matthew. The one between you and me.'

Stryker shoveled the last of the potatoes into his mouth. He kept his eyes on Rennick as he chewed. He swallowed and said, 'All right, King. It's hard to see a good man like you die, but as you will.'

King Rennick smiled. 'Thank you, Matthew. We feel it would be fair to all if we left Old Glory at noon. We'll walk up Corduroy Road toward the ketch pens. Wherever we meet is where the matter will be settled.'

'Noon, then. I and my deputy will be there.'

'Fine.'

'Breakfast? I've finished mine, but can always drink another cup of coffee.'

'Thank you, no. Mr Cahill has something ready for us in Bogtown.

'Until noon, then.'

Rennick smiled again. 'That's right, Matthew, all out in the open come noon.'

★ ★ ★

198

'*Patrón?*' Ramona stood at Fletcher Comstock's bedroom door.

'What is it?'

'*Patrón*. Miss Prudence. She did not come home last night. No one has been sleeping in her bed.'

'Prudence is a grown woman,' Comstock answered by reflex. Then he stopped. Prudence didn't stay out all night. It was not like her. 'No message?' he asked.

'No, *patrón*. What shall I do?'

Comstock forced himself to smile. 'Leave it to me, Ramona. I'll make sure Prudence is all right.'

'*Sí, patrón*.' The housekeeper made no move to leave.

'Something else, Ramona?'

'A man, *patrón*, I know not who, a man came. He said to give you this.' Ramona held out a white envelope.

'Why can't they wait until office hours,' Comstock grumbled. He took the envelope and held it up to the light. It definitely had something inside. He tore off one end and shook the paper out. He unfolded the single sheet and read the message.

I have your sister. If you want to see her alive, prepare a demand bank draft for $10,000. Put it in an envelope and place it in a copy of the Examiner. Have the house-keeper walk Main Street until someone asks her for the paper.

Comstock froze. Only one person could do something like this. Nate Cahill. Comstock remembered the night Cahill had come for the marshal's badge. Clearly he thought Comstock was a businessman, a desk jockey, one who let money do his talking for him. Cahill had a thing or two to learn.

'No breakfast, Ramona,' Comstock said.

'*Sí, patrón.*'

Comstock stripped the cravat from his neck and took off the linen shirt. He pulled off his leather boots and shucked the dark wool trousers. From the chest of drawers he took a plaid lumberman's shirt and donned it, followed by a pair of denim Levis and a short black leather vest. He selected a pair of lace-up forestry boots and laced his jeans inside them. He shifted his wallet, pocket watch, and loose coins to the pockets of his jeans and vest. The only thing he didn't change was his four-by-four Stetson.

As he prepared to leave the house, he stopped at the gun cabinet, where he retrieved a black gun belt with twin walnut-handled .44 Colt Frontier revolvers, model 1873, in black holsters. Comstock slung the gun belt around his waist and buckled it. He settled the unfamiliar weight of the guns on his hips and tilted their handles forward. He checked each pistol and added a sixth cartridge to each. Ready, he strode from the house, down Ash Street, across Corduroy Road and on to Main, where he turned right and walked to the marshal's office.

Matt Stryker looked up as Comstock rapped on the doorframe. 'Enter who dares,' he said with a smile. 'My, you're loaded for bear. Sorry, but you'll have to leave the guns here if you're going to walk around town.'

Comstock held out the note. 'Cahill's gone too far, Matt.'

'Looks like it. King Rennick and his boys are here to kill me. Now this. First things first. Rennick's coming out at noon. Once the fracas with him is over, you can go after Cahill.'

'Who's standing up to Rennick and them?'

'Me, and maybe Brady.' Stryker said nothing of Tom Hall.

'And Rennick?'

'I reckon there will be three — him, Kid McQueen, and Ace Tyler. That about evens things up.'

'I'll stand with you.'

'No, you won't. You've got the most important business in this town to run. Lots of people depend on you, so you shouldn't go get yourself shot and killed.'

'Cahill can't do this to me.'

'Cahill won't be with Rennick. Don't you worry about standing up to him. It's Cahill you need to reckon with. Do you hear me?'

Comstock took a deep breath. 'I hear you. The minute Rennick's out of the way, I'm after Cahill.'

'So be it.'

'Rennick's nowhere in Ponderosa,' Dan said from the doorway. 'I've been round the whole town. He's not there.'

'I saw him at breakfast,' Stryker said.

'Oh? What did he say?'

'Him and his boys will walk out from Old Glory at noon. They're coming up Corduroy towards Ponderosa. They expect me to meet them out there.'

'And me,' Dan said.

'It's my fight. You don't have to go,' Stryker said.

Dan tapped his badge with a forefinger. 'I'm law in this town. Just like you. I got the right to stand.'

Stryker looked Dan in the eye. 'It'll get hot.'

'I been practicing.'

'It ain't how fast you get the gun out, it's whether you hit anything when you pull the trigger.'

'I been practicing.' Dan's jaw set with determination. 'They kill you, they gotta kill me, too. That's the only way, and it's the right way.'

At last Stryker smiled, the scars stretching his face out of line. 'All right, Dan. It's your fight, too. Now, let's get ready. Fletcher, if you'll excuse us. Oh, and Fletcher, leave your guns here when you go.

'You take the Greener, Dan. It only gives you two shots, and don't you pull both triggers at once. Ace Tyler favors a shotgun, too, but his is sawed off. With the Greener, you'll have more range.

'So I get Tyler.'

'Hit him with one barrel. If that doesn't do the job, use the other one. Then drop the Greener and use your Colt on whoever is still standing. Once King and his rowdies are down, we move into Old Glory. Cahill's grabbed Miss Comstock — show him that note,

Fletcher — and he figures Fletcher will pay to get her back. Take down anyone of that bunch you see — Cahill, Wynn, Morales, Breed. Everything clear?'

'Yep. How much time we got?'

Stryker pulled a watch from his vest pocket. 'It's quarter of eleven right now.'

'I'll give the Greener a quick clean-up.'

'Dan, take the extra Colt. You won't have time to reload, probably.'

Dan Brady got the box with gun oil and rags from the cabinet and sat down with the Greener 10-gauge. 'I hear you, Marshal. You taking the sawed-off?'

'No. King and the Kid will have pistols. Ace will be the only shotgunner. King's honorable when it comes to gunfights. He'll come walking and won't stop until one of us is down.'

'I still think I should go,' said Comstock. 'Cahill's got Prudence.'

'You hold back, Fletcher. King Rennick's a job for the law. Once we've taken care of that problem, you can help find your sister.'

Dan rammed an oily rag through the barrels of the Greener, then switched to a dry cloth to remove any extra oil. He thumbed two shells into the shotgun and snapped it closed. 'OK,' he said, standing the Greener in the gun cabinet. He drew his Dragoon and ejected the cartridges into his hat.

'You're going to a gunfight with that antique?' asked Comstock.

Dan kept his attention on cleaning the revolver. 'Mr Comstock, sir,' he said, 'this here six-gun is old, but I keep good care of it and it sure shoots right where I point it. Yes, sir. I'm taking my Dragoon.' He wiped each cartridge as he replaced it into the Dragoon's cylinder, then added a sixth one. Replacing the huge gun into its holster, Dan got a .45 Colt Peacemaker from the drawer of the gun cabinet and proceeded to clean it, too. After carefully cleaning and replacing the cartridges, again adding a sixth one, he shoved the Peacemaker behind his belt in the small of his back. 'I'm ready, Marshal,' he said.

The watch showed 11.37.

Stryker wiped down his own six-gun and a second one he took from the desk. Both were .44 Colt Frontier revolvers. He loaded the cylinders with six cartridges each. Twelve shots to take care of King Rennick and his men.

11.44.

'You walk on my left,' Stryker said to Dan. 'When the shooting starts, I'll jag left. You fire the shotgun, then skedaddle right, behind me. It's hard to hit a quick-moving target. But don't shoot on the run. You'll just waste bullets.'

'I got you, Marshal.'

11.48.

Stryker stood. He carefully tied his holster to his thigh. It wouldn't do for his gun to hang up. He stuck the spare revolver in his waistband where it was ready to his hand. He settled his hat on his head.

11.53.

'Let's go,' Stryker said.

'I'm ready, Marshal.' Dan's voice quavered a bit.

Stryker left his black frock coat hung over a chair. 'Sun's bright,' he said. 'Shouldn't be too cold.'

Dan ignored his mackinaw on its peg in the wall. He clamped his teeth tight and loosened the big Dragoon revolver in its holster. He took the Greener from the gun cabinet, broke it open, and checked the loads one last time.

Stryker led the way toward Corduroy Road with Dan two steps behind and off to the left. At the top of the grade, Stryker pulled out his watch. 'One minute to noon,' he said.

A moment later, the batwings of Old Glory swung open. King Rennick had also shed his coat. Kid McQueen was dressed as always in a flannel shirt and cowhide vest. Ace Tyler looked slovenly, but his shotgun gleamed, freshly cleaned and oiled. The three gunmen stepped off the porch of Old Glory and walked up Corduroy Road, three abreast.

Matt Stryker and Dan Brady started down the grade. Stryker walked swiftly; Dan lengthened his stride to keep up.

The hired gunmen splashed across the Bog Creek ford, spread out slightly, and began their walk of death, moving east on the road. Half a dozen onlookers pushed their way through the saloon's swinging doors.

Stryker's fast pace shortened the distance to King Rennick's gunfighters almost before they could ready themselves. Dan kept a dozen paces to Stryker's left. He eared back the hammers of the Greener. 'Not yet,' Stryker said in a low voice.

When the gunfighters were fifty feet away, Stryker shouted, 'King Rennick's my meat!' He suddenly sprinted directly at the suave gunman whose hand darted for the handle of a Remington Army thrust into his red waist sash. Stryker's Colt was out and yammering. Bullets smashed into Rennick's body, lifting him to his toes and toppling him to the ground as his revolver crashed — once, twice, three times — the bullets digging holes in the hard surface of Corduroy Road.

Both Kid McQueen and Ace Tyler aimed at Matt Stryker, but he had already changed directions, darting to his left.

As the shooting started, Dan dropped to the ground and rolled twice to the right. He came to rest on his belly with the Greener pointed at Ace Tyler who had triggered a barrel at Stryker and missed. Dan licked his lips and touched off a barrel. The Greener kicked back against his shoulder and sent a load of buckshot smashing into Ace Tyler's side, turning him away just as he triggered the second barrel of his sawed-off. Dan rolled away and came up on one knee, the Greener pointing in Tyler's direction. The gunman was down, his dirty shirt tinged with blood. He clawed at the revolver in his waistband, murderous eyes on Dan, then pushed himself into a sitting position. Tyler raised the six-gun as if it weighed twenty pounds, but the second barrel of the Greener bellowed before Tyler could get a shot off. The buckshot took him full in the chest. He threw his arms wide and went over onto his back. Ignoring Tyler, Dan pulled the heavy dragoon Colt from its holster, cocking the hammer as he brought the weapon up. Hot lead burned a crease across his shoulder, but it bothered him no more than a mosquito bite. He looked over the killing ground. Tyler down and unmoving. Rennick curled in a ball on the ground. Matt Stryker standing spraddle-legged, exchanging shots with Kid McQueen. Dan ran toward the marshal, who dropped his .44 and drew his spare.

'Get the Kid,' Stryker shouted at Dan. The deputy stopped, lifted the big Dragoon as if he were target practicing, took a long breath, and squeezed the trigger. Kid McQueen hollered as Dan's bullet took him in the right shoulder joint, smashing the youngster around and making him drop his gun.

'Good man,' Stryker said.

'Give up, Kid. This is no day for you to die,' the marshal said to the gunman.

The Kid nodded. 'You got me, Marshal. Can't hold a gun. Never was no good with my left.'

'Stryker!' It came almost as a scream. Stryker and Dan whipped around as one. King Rennick stood with his legs spread apart. Blood covered the front of his shirt and dripped from his trouser cuffs. He held a Remington with both hands. 'Damn you to Hell, Matthew. I swear, you're coming with me.' As he spoke, he pulled the trigger. The bullet took Stryker high in the chest, almost knocking him down. Rennick eared the hammer back and shot again. Stryker staggered and went to one knee. He raised the spare .44 and the sound of his firing blended with the roar of Dan Brady's Dragoon. Both bullets found Rennick, one entering his left eye and exiting in a cloud of bloody mist, the other catching him in the throat. The man they called King collapsed like a puppet with cut strings.

Kid McQueen sat down where he stood, his right arm hanging useless. He was no danger any longer. Stryker tried to stand but couldn't make it. 'Leave me be, son,' he said to Dan. 'I'll do. Find that girl.'

'I'll find her, Marshal, or I'll die making a try at it,' Dan said. He left Matt Stryker bleeding on the grass beside Corduroy Road and strode toward the swinging doors of Old Glory, ejecting empty shells from his Dragoon and replacing them with cartridges from his belt as he went. The onlookers scattered when he climbed the steps to the porch.

'Ca-a-a-hill!' he screamed, and charged through the batwings. A pistol shot cracked from within the saloon; its slug tore a chunk from the doorframe as Dan went through. He saw Morales with a smoking gun in his hand. Dan dived for the floor while taking an offhand shot at Morales to shake his aim. A bullet plowed into the hardwood floor not six inches in front of Dan's face. He fired the Dragoon like he would point his finger.

The bullet went true. It pierced Morales's brisket. He dropped his gun and splayed his fingers over the wound in his chest. '*Madré mia*,' he whispered as he sagged to the floor, the light dying from his eyes.

The back door flew open. Nate Cahill barged into the saloon with a shotgun. He looked wildly about, searching for a target. His eyes fell on Dan struggling to his feet. He raised the shotgun to his shoulder and a blast shook the saloon. Dan flinched, expecting a double dose of buckshot to nail him to the bar.

'Nate Cahill won't bother you no more, Deputy,' said Tom Hall, smoke curling from the twin barrels of the shotgun he had poked through the window.

At last Dan could scramble to his feet. He echoed Stryker's words. 'Leave me be, Tom. Go take care of the marshal. I'll find Miss Prudence.' Dan held his Dragoon at arm's length, aimed at Jigger the bartender. 'Pull the shotgun out, Jigger, and put it on the bar.'

Jigger did what he was told.

'Push it over here.'

He did.

Dan picked up the shotgun. 'Now just back off and stay put.'

Jigger hustled to the other end of the bar.

Dan held the shotgun muzzle up and emptied it into the ceiling. He'd have to go upstairs. He hoped Prudence would be there. The shotgun blast would give them something to think about. He reloaded the Dragoon. He had twelve shots for whatever came. He took a deep breath, walked to the back door, dragged Nate Cahill's body out of the way, and started up the back stairs.

12

Prudence finally fell asleep despite the cold, and woke only when the door creaked open. 'Who's there?' Her voice cracked. 'What do you want?'

She could only make out a dark shape in the glare from the door. A hard hand grasped her arm and pulled her to her feet. 'Ouch. You're hurting me,' she said.

'That right? How's this?' The hand twisted harder.

Prudence gasped.

'Hurt? Well, maybe you'll find out what hurt really means. Nate wants you upstairs. Come along.' Wynn Cahill cut the strips of canvas binding her ankles with a sharp Bowie. He jerked her forward. 'Move it!'

Prudence stumbled from the lean-to with Wynn holding tight to her arm. He steered her to the stairway at the back of Old Glory and forced her up the steps.

'Got the girl,' Wynn said at the door.

'Bring her in.'

At least it was warm in the room. Nate Cahill sat behind his grand mahogany desk. Breed leaned against the wall, his arms folded. He scowled. Morales stood beside the door.

'King will have Matt Stryker and that deputy taken care of at noon,' Cahill said. 'Morales, you head on down to the bar. Get Jigger to send something up for the girl. Once the law is out of the way, Comstock will come through with the money, sure.'

'*Sí*,' Morales said. He clumped down the stairs. A few moments later, Jake the bartender came with saleratus biscuits, some fried bacon, and a mug of coffee.

'Cut her loose,' Cahill said to Wynn.

Wynn's Bowie sliced the bonds from Prudence's wrists.

'Eat,' Cahill said.

'I couldn't,' Prudence said. 'I won't.'

'Suit yourself,' Wynn said. He back-handed her, his knuckles smashing into

217

her cheek. She fell into the easy chair behind her. The surprise of the blow kept her from crying out, but tears welled in her eyes as her hand went to her bruised and swelling face.

The sound of gunfire brought a smile to Cahill's face. 'That'll be King and his boys doing for the marshal,' he said. Shotguns crashed. Then pistol fire again. A short silence, then four pistol shots too close together to be one gun. Silence. Cahill looked at his brother. Both men wore huge grins. Breed hadn't moved an inch. He seemed to be watching Prudence.

'Ca-a-a-a-hill.' The scream came from the front door of Old Glory. A six-gun spoke, followed immediately by another.

'Damn,' Cahill said. 'King must not have got them all.' He snatched a sawed-off shotgun from the gun rack and checked its loads. 'Watch the girl,' he said. He threw open the door and pounded down the stairs. Wynn walked over and slapped Prudence across the face. Breed started. He seemed ready to draw his gun.

'You sit quiet, missy,' Wynn said. 'I'll take care of you later.'

Tears leaked from Prudence's eyes and ran down her cheeks.

A shotgun bellowed below. Then another. Buckshot came flying through the floor. Wynn jumped away. 'Goddam!' He started for the door when the sound of running footsteps came from the stairs. Wynn jerked his Colt from its holster. He stopped against the wall where the door would hide him when it opened. Breed stood with his arms folded as before. The door crashed wide and Dan Brady charged into the room.

'Dan! Watch out!' Prudence finally found her voice, but her warning came too late. Wynn Cahill stepped out from behind the door and clubbed Dan with the barrel of his Colt. Dan's Dragoon flew from his hand and skittered across the floor. He dropped to his hands and knees, but didn't go all the way down.

'Stand, if you can, deputy,' Wynn ordered.

Dan shook his head as if to clear it, then struggled to his feet.

Prudence looked at Dan, then at his Dragoon, then back at Dan. The gun was too far away.

Wynn jerked the Peacemaker from Dan's belt and tossed it after the Dragoon. He hit Dan lightly across the face with the barrel of his revolver. A three-inch gash opened up below Dan's cheekbone and splashed blood across his face. He staggered but didn't go down.

'Where's my brother, Deputy?' Wynn said.

Dan stood silent.

Wynn swung the revolver back across Dan's jaw. 'I asked you a question, asshole. Answer.'

Dan spit blood and mucus to the floor at Wynn's feet. He raised his face to look Wynn in the eye. 'Dead,' he said. 'Killed by Tom Hall's shotgun. You'd best let Miss Prudence go. King's bunch is dead or down. Morales is done for. No one to back your play now, bad man. Give it up.'

'I've got you!' Wynn screamed. 'I've got her! You all are going to wish you was never born before I get through with you.'

Prudence looked at the Dragoon again. Was there a chance she could reach it?

'You just stand right there, Mr Deputy. I got just the thing for you.' Wynn sidestepped around Cahill's mahogany desk. He opened a drawer and rummaged about for something. 'Ah, there it is.' He showed Dan a ridged lump of lead. 'This here fits right in your fist, you see. This here is what happened to Stryker's face. Let's see what it can do to yours.' Wynn shifted his revolver to his left hand and grasped the lump of lead with his right. Two long steps back around the desk and a looping right to Dan's ear. Dan went down but clambered up again just in time to meet Wynn's fist to his jaw. As he crumpled, Prudence leaped across the floor, scrambling for the cocked

Dragoon Colt that lay half under the desk. She stretched her right hand out as she dived and her fingers closed on the handle of the big gun.

'Damn you, bitch,' Wynn shouted. He dropped the lump of lead and tossed his Colt from left hand to right.

Desperately, Prudence struggled to bring the heavy Dragoon into line.

Wynn cocked his Peacemaker. 'You're dead meat, whore,' he said, raising the Colt toward Prudence.

Suddenly Breed moved. His hand blurred to the gun at his side and in less than a quarter of a second it belched fire and its slug took Wynn Cahill through the left bicep, pierced his chest, plowed through the back side of his heart, nicked his spine, and slithered along his ribs to exit behind his right arm.

'Wha — ' Wynn dropped to the floor, his mouth working like a landed carp.

'You don't shoot women,' Breed said. Wynn didn't reply. He was dead.

Boots sounded on the stairs and

Fletcher Comstock burst through the door to find two gunbarrels aimed at his gut. Breed held one with casual confidence. Prudence held the other with both hands, her legs curled under her and her back against the desk.

'Whoa, whoa. I'm friendly,' Comstock said. 'I'm going to put my guns away. Don't get sudden.'

Dan heaved himself to his hands and knees. 'Good to see you, Mr Comstock,' he said in a small voice. 'Breed saved Miss Prudence. You leave him be.'

'Never shot a man who had the drop on me.' Comstock shoved his Colts back in their holsters.

'It's been done,' Breed said. 'My cousin Garet Havelock got Juanito O'Rourke when he had the drop.'

'Havelock's your cousin?'

'Mother's side.'

'Jeez.'

Comstock offered Dan a hand. Dan grasped it and let Comstock pull him to his feet. 'How's Marshal Stryker?' he asked.

'Hit pretty hard, but he'll live. That's

what Doc Huntly says anyway.'

'Tom?'

'He's with the marshal.'

Breed helped Prudence to her feet. 'This is yours,' she said, holding the Dragoon out to Dan.

'Yeah. Looked for a minute like you were gonna save my bacon with that abbreviated cannon I carry around on my hip.'

'I hope you carry it a long time,' Prudence said. 'I'll feel safer.'

★ ★ ★

GUNS OF PONDEROSA SAVE INNOCENT LIVES

Gunfire erupted near the GW&SF ketch pens on Corduroy Road as Ponderosa's intrepid lawmen met and subdued killers hired by the infamous Nate Cahill. The conflict began moments after noon on the day before yesterday when the killers, identified by onlookers as

King Rennick, Kid McQueen, and Ace Tyler, began shooting at Marshal Matthew Stryker and Deputy Daniel Brady.

When the gunsmoke cleared, those observing saw Rennick and Tyler on the ground lifeless. Kid McQueen had been shot through the shoulder by Deputy Brady. He will live but may never regain the use of his right arm. Marshal Stryker was wounded in the action, suffering shots to his chest and shoulder. Doctor Vernon Huntly's opinion is that Marshal Stryker will live.

Said Cahill held Miss Prudence Comstock prisoner and attempted to extort $10,000 from her brother Fletcher Comstock of Comstock Log and Lumber Company with that fact. Following the gunfight at Corduroy Road, Deputy Brady invaded Nate Cahill's stronghold, the saloon Old Glory, where he shot and killed Juan Morales, one of Cahill's band of outlaws, and where Deputy Thomas Hall shot and killed Nate Cahill himself before he could shoot Deputy Brady.

Miss Comstock was held prisoner in the room above Old Glory. Deputy Brady proceeded to that room, searching for Miss Comstock. The room was occupied by Cahill's brother Wynn Cahill, Miss Comstock, who Cahill was determined to abuse, and Seth Graffunder, who is also known as Breed. The younger Cahill disarmed Deputy Brady and began to beat him. In the melee Miss Comstock attempted to reach a discarded revolver with which to dispatch the younger Cahill. Cahill turned his own pistol on Miss Comstock and would have murdered her if not for Mr Graffunder, a relative of US Marshal Havelock, who shot and killed Wynn Cahill. Thanks to our intrepid lawmen, Ponderosa is once more safe for ordinary citizen.

Dan Brady made the rounds at night; once just after dusk, once about midnight. Rolly Parsons took over Old Glory and seemed to be running a reasonable operation. The rule against weapons in Ponderosa still held, and Dan made it stick. He'd come away from the gunfight at Corduroy a harder man. His mild manner made some newcomers misjudge him, but if they stepped across the line, he came down hard. The old Dragoon he still carried was just as effective at buffaloing wayward cowboys and bluejacket soldiers as Matt Stryker's Frontier Colt.

As soon as Stryker was out of danger, Tom Hall disappeared. Prudence Comstock visited Stryker's room in the hotel almost every day, as did Dan Brady and Fletcher Comstock. Becky Clark brought his meals and charged the town for them.

Two weeks after the gunfight, Stryker got out of bed. 'Can't heal while I'm on my back,' he said, and he began taking walks up and down the boardwalk,

227

stopping in and talking with merchants and business people and generally making a nuisance of himself, according to Prudence, but he never wore a badge.

Stryker entered Clark's Kitchen at midmorning when he knew Fletcher Comstock would be there.

'Good morning, Fletcher,' he said. 'Mind if I join you?'

Comstock shoved a chair out with his foot. 'Help yourself.'

Stryker sat. 'Coffee, if you would, Becky,' he called.

'Be right there,' came the reply from the kitchen. Becky appeared with a coffee pot in one hand and a plate of doughnuts and a mug in the other. 'Here's some grease for your conversation,' she said, setting the plate and mug on the table. 'Good to see you up and about, Matt. Healing well?'

'Still sore, Becky, but I'm mending.'

'Good, good,' she said, as she poured the coffee. 'Holler if you need anything.' She disappeared back into the kitchen, leaving Stryker and Comstock alone in the restaurant.

Stryker took a sip of his coffee. 'I swear that woman makes the best coffee this side of New Orleans. Too bad she's married.'

'What's on your mind, Matt?'

Stryker sat silent for a long moment. 'It's time for me to move on, Fletcher. The problem you hired me to take care of is over. It's time.'

Comstock sighed. 'I'd try to talk you into staying, but I know how stubborn you can get. When do you figure to leave?'

'No need to hang around. I can ride. I'll leave day after tomorrow. But I want to settle one thing before I go.'

'Pay?'

'No. I know you're good for that.'

'What, then?'

'I want you to give the marshal's badge and a hundred a month to Dan Brady.'

Comstock's eyebrows shot up. 'Brady?'

'He's as good a man as you'll get,

Fletcher. You saw how he stood at Corduroy. You've seen how he's handled this town since. He's the one you need, Fletcher. I'll stake my name on it.'

'Need to talk to the others first.'

'Ponderosa Club?'

'Yep.'

'Do it. But I'd like to ride out of here knowing Ponderosa is in good hands.'

Two days later, Comstock accompanied Matt Stryker to the marshal's office. Breed sat in one of the high-back chairs with a cup of coffee balanced on his knee. Dan Brady took his feet off the desk drawer and sat up straight when he saw Stryker enter.

'Good day, Marshal,' he said. 'Things are quiet in Ponderosa and Bogtown's no more than a dull roar.'

'That's good, Dan. That's good. Fletcher here's got something for you.'

Fletcher Comstock stepped forward and held his hand out across the desk. 'The town would like you to wear this badge, Dan,' he said. 'Matt Stryker recommends you, and I've personally seen how you conducted yourself since the fight at Corduroy. The job pays a hundred a month and found. Will you take it?'

The broad grin on Dan's face was nearly answer enough. 'I will on one condition,' he said.

'What's that?'

Dan's grin got wider. 'I'll do the job for seventy-five a month if you'll take the twenty-five and add it to the usual twenty-five and found a deputy earns.'

Both Comstock and Stryker looked puzzled.

'I want to hire me a good deputy, and I reckon that'll cost fifty a month.'

'Got anyone in mind?'

'Yes, if you authorize the pay.'

'All right,' Comstock said. 'Hire yourself a deputy.'

'Thank you. I accept the job.' Dan took the badge from Comstock and removed his deputy's badge to replace it with the marshal's star in a circle.

'I'll be leaving, Dan,' Stryker said.

'I'll likely be seeing you around. Until I do, take care.'

Dan came from behind the desk with his hand outstretched. 'Thank you, Matt Stryker,' he said, and clasped Stryker's hand. 'You taught me what it's like to be a lawman. I'm beholden. Ride loose in the saddle.'

'I will,' Stryker said. 'Rely on your own judgment, Dan. You've got the right ideas. I'll just be moving on. See you. You, too, Breed.'

Breed put a finger to his hat brim in salute.

After Stryker and Comstock left, Dan turned to Breed. 'Graf,' he said, 'I'd be obliged if you'd take this deputy's badge. The job pays fifty a month and found.'

Breed grinned. 'Graf, is it? I like that. Be good to work with you, Dan Brady. I'm getting to like Ponderosa more all the time.'

Brady handed Breed the badge. 'I'll be wanting the evening off on Saturday. I hear Cory Cooley's giving a dance at the White House. You can watch the town.'

Dan hitched at the gunbelt holding the heavy Dragoon. Maybe Miss Prudence would like to go to that dance. He left the office and walked down the board-walk toward the *Examiner*.

THE END

We do hope that you have enjoyed reading this large print book.

Did you know that all of our titles are available for purchase?

We publish a wide range of high quality large print books including:
Romances, Mysteries, Classics
General Fiction
Non Fiction and Westerns

Special interest titles available in large print are:
The Little Oxford Dictionary
Music Book, Song Book
Hymn Book, Service Book

Also available from us courtesy of Oxford University Press:
Young Readers' Dictionary
(large print edition)
Young Readers' Thesaurus
(large print edition)

For further information or a free brochure, please contact us at:
Ulverscroft Large Print Books Ltd.,
The Green, Bradgate Road, Anstey,
Leicester, LE7 7FU, England.
Tel: (00 44) **0116 236 4325**
Fax: (00 44) **0116 234 0205**